Praise for *I Want to Show You*

"[With its] impressive agility and inventiveness . . . *I Want to Show You More* is an obsessive first collection that feels like a fifth or sixth. . . . Provides the most engaging literary treatment of Christianity since [Flannery] O'Connor, without a hint of the condescension the subject often receives in contemporary fiction. . . . [Quatro's] flights of fancy are never ostentatious or arbitrary; instead they grow naturally out of the emotional and psychological states of her characters. Readers may hope to see more of this hallucinatory mode from her, but—if they're like me—they will welcome whatever they can get."
— J. Robert Lennon, *The New York Times Book Review*

"Quatro has a poet's compound eye . . . [and] fearless lyricism. . . . Expansive, joyful, with forgiveness supplanting ruination. Who needs the New Testament? In Quatro's world, hard Genesis is always making way for the softer Song of Solomon: 'I sat down under his shadow with great delight, and his fruit was sweet to my taste.'"
— James Wood, *The New Yorker*

"Quatro's language is admirably light on its feet. Hers is the consummate prose that doesn't call attention to itself with verbosity or sparsity. Her descriptions are simple, selective, and always hit their mark."
— Kelsey Joseph, *Los Angeles Review of Books*

"Quatro very much establishes her own distinctive voice and style. . . . A luminous collection."   — S. Kirk Walsh, *San Francisco Chronicle*

"Quatro's stories [have] led some to compare her work to that of Walker Percy and Flannery O'Connor. I also picked up metal-detector traces of Jayne Anne Phillips . . . and of Lorrie Moore's pulverizing wit. . . . In order to be good at big things, writers must be good at small ones. Quatro's details resonate. . . . There's so much in these stories that's shocking. Yet there's so much solace."
— Dwight Garner, *The New York Times*

"[An] impressive debut about the shortcomings of people who wrestle with angels, and usually lose."   —Amy Gentry, *Chicago Tribune*

"Quatro is so good that we'll temper any eye rolling at the usual 'voice of a new generation' claims with the hope that the title of this debut collection isn't just a tease."   —Julie Vadnal, *Elle*

"[A] fresh, forward collection . . . the best of her stories carry a brazen authority."   — Rebecca Bengal, *Vogue*

"Occasionally, a first book of short stories can shake the world awake with its extraordinarily singular vision and voice, reinvigorating language. Jamie Quatro's *I Want to Show You More* is such a book—and holy fuck, is it. . . . Startling, heartrending, and extraordinarily sexy . . . [with] allegorical scene[s] worthy of Kafka or Donald Barthelme."
        —Baynard Woods, *Baltimore City Paper*

"Some stories are uncomfortable, pushing the limit with their sheer oddity and disregard for social norms. But isn't that the point?"
        —Lindsay Deutsch, *USA Today* (★ ★ ★)

"These stories are bold (and wise) . . . Many comparisons will be made between Quatro's and Flannery O'Connor's treatments of religion and faith; they are all accurate and deserved. But this book pushes past that inheritance by examining how it holds up it in our time."
        —Jennine Capó Crucet, *The L Magazine*

"Quatro has accomplished a rare paradox: [Her] collection is stitched together and yet it's loose and baggy, letting in a lot of surprise."
        —Nina Schuyler, The Rumpus

"Deeply intriguing . . . Subtly metamorphosing . . . Shimmers with touches of Flannery O'Connor and George Saunders . . . [Quatro's] compelling moral dilemmas yoke bizarreness with authenticity."
        —Donna Seaman, *Booklist*

"[Quatro's] stories are uncensored, sometimes eccentric explorations of life—its darkness and brilliance." —*Oxford American*

"With her wild and dark imagination, Quatro has crafted highly original, thought-provoking, and deeply moving stories about faith, marriage, infidelity, sex, and death. This is bold, daring fiction." —*The Columbus Dispatch*

"A remarkable debut by an important new voice . . . Quatro [has] a mature understanding of how we handle disappointment and how, quite often, we take refuge in the most unhelpful places." —Patrick Ryan, *The Toronto Star*

"Like George Saunders, she's in tune with the warped patois of twenty-first-century life, holy, precious, teeming with energy, but clear only in contradiction." —*The American | In Italia*

"I knew when I read this collection that it was going to be one of my favorite books of the year. . . . Quatro's short stories are knock-your-socks-off good, and they deserve every bit of praise they're garnering. I've run out of ways to say THIS BOOK IS GOOD GO READ IT, so just do it, OK?" —Rebecca Joines Schinsky, Book Riot

"From under the placid surface of Quatro's stories sentences of astonishing strangeness startle the pond and serve as reminders of the dangerous, unknowable human heart. . . . Here is a new talent with work made to last." —Christine Schutt

"A brilliant new voice in American fiction has arrived. Bright, sharp, startling, utterly distinctive, passionate, and secretive, Quatro's stories are missives from deep within the landscape of American womanhood. . . . She has earned a place alongside Amy Hempel, Lydia Davis, and Alice Munro." —David Means

"Exquisitely crafted, the characters here are as complex, real, and finely drawn as you'll find. No hyperbole here: Jamie Quatro is an outstanding new talent." —Elizabeth Crane

"Fasten your seat belt: Jamie Quatro is a writer of great talent who knows how to take a dark turn without ever tapping the brakes and then bring you back into daylight with breathtaking precision. These amazing stories explore the human boundaries between the physical world and the spiritual—lust, betrayal, and loss in perfect balance with love, redemption, and grace." —Jill McCorkle

"These are stories that make you stop whatever you're doing and read. They show us who we are at our better moments and those other moments too. These are delightful stories for this brand new century, from an author unafraid to face it. I salute a brilliant new American writer." —Tom Franklin

"The characters in these absolutely unique stories live at a nearly intolerable level of intensity, stretched on a self-created rack between faith and sexuality—and they're even smart enough to be conflicted about whether or not there's a conflict. Jamie Quatro spares us neither the strangeness of their experience nor its discomfiting familiarity. She observes them with a cool, comic yet compassionate eye, and shapes the raw material of their passionate strivings with a steady, skillful hand—a miracle in which any reader can believe." —David Gates

"Jamie Quatro's stories are about religion and children and sex and death and infidelity and God, and together they create one of the most authentically horrifying portraits of modern American adulthood I've ever read. Did I mention these stories are also very, very funny? Ladies and gentlemen, this is what short fiction is for." —Tom Bissell

"Quatro has mastered the art of the double take—that whiplash of recognition that gets the reader first at the level of the sentence, then, with extra reward, at story's end. The author pushes fearlessly, cape close to horns, blade held high and at risky angles. An impressive debut." —Sven Birkerts

"I keep saying, 'God almighty, that's a great story' after I finish one."
—George Singleton

I Want to
Show You
More

I Want to Show You More

Stories by Jamie Quatro

Grove Press
New York

This is a work of fiction. Although Lookout Mountain exists, the names, characters, and incidents in the work are the product of the author's imagination or are used fictitiously.

These stories originally appeared in slightly different form in the following publications: "Caught Up" in *Tin House*; "Decomposition: A Primer for Promiscuous Housewives" in *American Short Fiction*; "Ladies and Gentlemen of the Pavement" in *The Cincinnati Review*; "Here" in *The Hopkins Review*; "What Friends Talk About" in *The Southern Review*; "1.7 to Tennessee" and "Holy Ground" in *The Antioch Review*; "The Anointing" in *Guernica*; "Imperfections", "You Look Like Jesus", and "Relatives of God" in *AGNI*; "Better to Lose an Eye" in *Blackbird*; "Georgia the Whole Time" in *Alaska Quarterly Review* (formerly "Up 58 South"); "Sinkhole" in *Ploughshares*; and *The PEN/O.Henry Prize Stories 2013*; "Demolition" in *The Kenyon Review*.

Printed in the United States of America
Published simultaneously in Canada

ISBN-13: 978-0-8021-2223-0
eBook ISBN: 978-0-8021-9374-2

Grove Press
an imprint of Grove/Atlantic, Inc.
154 West 14th Street
New York, NY 10011

Distributed by Publishers Group West

www.groveatlantic.com

14 15 16 17   10 9 8 7 6 5 4 3 2 1

To Scott

Just once in my life—oh, when have I ever wanted
anything just once in my life?

—Amy Hempel, *"Memoir"*

CONTENTS

I Want to
Show You
More

CAUGHT UP

The vision started coming when I was nine. It was always the same: I was alone, standing on the brick patio in front of our house, watching thick clouds above the mountains turn shades of red and purple, then draw themselves together and spiral. Whirlpool, hurricane, galaxy. The wind picked up, my hair whipped my face, and I felt—knew—that the world was on the cusp of a cataclysm. Then came a tugging in my middle, as if I were a kite about to be yanked up by a string attached just below my navel. Takeoff was imminent; all I had to do was surrender—close my eyes, relax my limbs—and I would be catapulted, belly-first, into the vortex.

The vision ended there. I never left the patio.

When I told my mother, she said, God speaks to his children in dreams. She said we should always be ready for the Lord's return: lead a clean life and stay busy with our work, keeping an eye skyward. I pictured my mother up on our roof, sitting in a folding chair, snapping beans.

I don't remember when the vision stopped coming. Somewhere along the way I forgot about it. I grew up and married a

1

good man who cries at baptisms and makes our children carry spiders outside instead of smashing them; who never goes to sleep without kissing some part of my body. He says he wants to know, on his deathbed, that his lips have touched every square inch. In grad school, when I told him I was attracted to one of his friends who'd made a pass at me, he said, "Show me what you would do with him, if you could."

Three years ago—seventeen years into this marriage—I fell in love with a man who lives nine hundred miles away. Ten months of talking daily with this man, until finally he bought train tickets and arranged a meeting date. We'll just—pick a car, he said on the phone. Any car, so long as it's empty.

The day he suggested this, I called my mother and told her about the affair. I told her I wanted the infidelity to stop, but planned to keep the man as a friend. I said I loved my husband and wanted to protect my marriage. What I didn't say was that I only knew I was *supposed* to want to protect it; thought that if I did the right thing, eventually my heart would follow.

My mother was quiet.

Please tell me you won't keep him, she said. In any way.

Are the children all right? she said. Can you put one of them on?

After we hung up, I went for a long run, then walked the last block up our street's steep incline. A cloud covered the sun so the entire length of pavement was in shade, and then the cloud pulled back, all at once; the light sped down the street toward me, and in those few seconds it looked like the road itself was moving, a conveyor belt that would scoop me up from underneath. The old vision returned. The upward tug in my belly. I recognized the feeling—what I felt every time the other man, the faraway man, told me what he would do if he had me in person, my wrists pinned over my head.

It would be devotional, he'd said. I would lay myself on your tongue like a Communion wafer.

This time, in the vision, the other man was with me. I would like to say he was standing beside me—that we were equals—but he was the size of a toddler. I was holding him. He was limp and barely breathing, his skin gray, the color of my two-year-old son's face the night we rushed him to the ER for croup, and I knew the reason I was about to be *caught up* was because I was supposed to carry the man to God and lay him in His lap so that God could . . . what? I didn't know.

Bullshit, the man said when I told him about the vision. I'm already there.

My turn, he said. You, me, walking in the woods. It's winter. We've just had two feet of snow. We're playing together like kids. I'm chasing you, and when I catch you, I push you into a drift and lie on top of you. Above us the sky rips open and God is there, smiling down, and what he is saying, over and over, is *Yes*.

I wish I knew God your way, I said.

You will, he said. All you have to do is show up. Grand Central, February thirteenth, nine A.M.

Tell me you'll be there, he said.

Two years later, when I called my mother to tell her how much I missed the man, how on the one hand I wished I had gone through with our planned meeting yet at the same time regretted even the phone sex, because if we hadn't done *that* we might have been able to save the friendship; when I told her that something inside me was weeping all the time, and

3

that I hoped there would be a literal Second Coming and Consummated Kingdom because then the man and I could spend eternity just talking, she said, Wait—phone sex? And I said, I thought I told you, and she said, You told me you had an affair, and I said, No I didn't, we didn't, not in that way, and she said, I must have assumed, and I said, I can't believe all this time you've been thinking I went through with it.

You might as well have, she said. It's all the same in God's eyes.

DECOMPOSITION:
A *Primer for*
Promiscuous Housewives

I: Algor Mortis: early postmortem stage in which the body gradually loses heat to the ambient environment.

Two weeks before Christmas your husband says, Let's take a walk through Rock City, and you say, Sure, let's, though at this point neither of you cares about seeing the Enchanted Trail with its twenty thousand glittering lights. You park at the coffee shop across the street and go in for a cup of Yogi Calm, choosing this flavor not because you're about to kill the man you've been having an affair with (you don't know this yet), but because you think *calm* sounds nice this time of year, and they're out of the chinaberry/jasmine, and it's too late in the day for caffeine.

You skip the lights and walk up Fleetwood, which curves around behind Rock City. It's a clear night, cold enough to see your breath. Your husband is silent. You pass the churning pump shed and the owner's house, a yellow Cape Cod with four dormers—three identical, the fourth oddly elongated with an arched transom—thinking, as you always do when you pass this house, that the incongruity must make sense from the inside.

At the back of the albino deer enclosure you and your husband pause to look over the stucco wall. None of the deer are out. You take a sip of tea and it's so hot the skin peels from the roof of your mouth, and it's this sensation you'll come to associate with the moment, after months of lying, you finally decide to answer your husband's question truthfully.

You're in love with him, aren't you.

Yes, you say, probing a delicate strip of scalded tissue with the tip of your tongue.

When you get home your four children are sprawled in front of the new flatscreen. They're watching a SpongeBob episode in which Patrick runs halfway up a mountain, falls off, then repeats the action, each time hoping he'll make it to the top.

Upstairs, your husband says to them, then goes into the bedroom and closes the door, so it's up to you to pay the babysitter, manage the teeth-brushing, book-reading, bedtime-praying, hall light–adjusting.

Tell Daddy to come up, your six-year-old daughter says. I want a kiss from Daddy.

Your husband is curled into the fetal position on his side of the king-sized bed. Beside him, lying faceup, is the man with whom you've been having the distance affair. You're not surprised to see the other man in this particular spot—in your mind he's been interjecting himself along this length of bed for the past ten months. Your husband's shoulders are quivering and you know you should say or do something to comfort him but you're shocked to discover that your only concern is for the man in the center of the mattress.

You lie down on your side of the bed, gently touch the man's forehead to wake him up and tell him that the time has come to say goodbye. The skin is cooler than it should be.

You sit up. Feel the man's cheeks, chest, arms. He's cold everywhere. You straddle the body, thinking *ABC* (remembering, only fleetingly, how often you'd imagined yourself in exactly this position) but he must have taken his last breath while you were out walking, because a) the airway is clear but b) he is not breathing and c) you cannot induce circulation even after twenty minutes of CPR.

You collapse beside the man, wrap your warm hand around one of his, the fingers already so stiff you have to push them down.

You knew your confession would do this.

You thought it would happen gradually.

What does he do for you that I can't, your husband says.

The following day is marked by a strange but not unwelcome sense of peace. Chicken broth, lit candles, hot baths. Enya's *Winter* album. There is a sweetness, a rightness, a bigger-than-yourselfness to the day. Under different circumstances you would call it a holiness. The death is as it should be, you know this intellectually; in fact, the overall intellectual quality of your mood is striking, the absence of raw feeling; though you've read about grief, and know that shock is the earliest stage, so you wonder if you truly feel nothing or if you feel so much it is beyond the capacity of a human body to process it, the nervous system therefore—immediately, mercifully—converting every rising emotion into a sensation of nothingness.

The sun is out. Dark branches splay themselves against an ecstatic blue. You decide to take a long drive, alone, on the one-lane highway that leads out the back of Lookout Mountain. Fresh snow bends limbs on the Georgia pines, narrowing the road, making it intimate.

You tell God you're grateful he has taken the burden of sin from you. You know it's the right thing to say.

In the front yard you pick clusters of holly and magnolia to arrange on the pillow around the man's head, thinking the least you can do is create a little beauty around the edges of death. But when you enter the bedroom you notice the man's skin has turned the color of wet newspaper. You smell menthol and burnt plastic and something like rotten Nilla wafers. You hold your breath and close your eyes while the word *inaccessible* lights up against the backs of your eyelids—the thing you wanted there in front of you but also as far away as the bottom of the ocean—and you remember how your husband said, when you were pregnant with your first child, *inches from us but she might as well be on another planet,* and it is perhaps this realization—you are *shut out*—that makes you drop the leaves onto the wood floor, grab the bedpost and hold on and say, to your husband, still curled up on his side of the bed: But I wanted him.

I checked the body out, your husband says. It's fucking wax.

He sits up.

You didn't think it was real, did you?

You and your husband meet with your pastor, who comes over after you've put the children to bed. He brings his wife. The two of them somehow manage to look both grave and jovial (*infidelity is serious; all is forgiven*). You sit in the living room. You've dimmed the lights. Before anyone speaks you hand the pastor your confession, which you've typed because a) you will cry if forced to speak and b) you want to spare your husband hearing the details one more time and c) you feel the confession is authentic and moving, that it has literary merit, and perhaps the pastor could use it to help others in similar situations, or even reference it in a sermon, and in this way the anguish you've created might acquire meaning.

We're standing on holy ground, the pastor begins.

You weep.

Confessions of this kind tend to trickle out, he says. New bits of information can leak for months, which slows the healing process. If there's anything you haven't told your husband, now's the time.

You ask if you could please have your confession back. Read aloud the bits about the texts, the recordings of your voice you created using GarageBand, the nude photos you e-mailed. The phone sex.

Like Jacob, the pastor says when you finish, you have wrestled with God and overcome. But make no mistake: those who wrestle come away wounded.

You will walk with a limp for the rest of your life, the pastor says.

You don't know if he means you or your husband.

II: Bloat: in which gases associated with anaerobic metabolism accumulate, creating enough pressure to force liquids from the eyes, nose, mouth, ears, and anus.

Go to classroom parties. Help your four-year-old make a gingerbread house out of a milk carton and graham crackers. Admire his roof, onto which he crowds the entire Dixie-cupful of gumdrops and peppermint disks. Comfort him when the roof slides off; wipe his nose, encourage a more balanced distribution of candy.

Shower, shave legs, apply makeup. Attend your husband's departmental Christmas party. Force the eggnog and candy cane–shaped cookies. Listen to yourself say, over and over: Yes, four *is* a lot of work, but it's also a lot of fun.

Stuff envelopes with the annual letter in which you have the children answer a sharing question: What does Christmas mean to you? What do you want from Santa? If you could change one thing about the world, what would it be?

Decorate the tree with the ornaments you've purchased for your children, one per child per year, dates written in Sharpie on ballerina feet and bunny ears, hockey sticks and electric guitars with tensile fishing-line strings.

Help the six-year-old wire the pinecone angel the two of you made to the top of the tree.

Do not forget to take pictures.

I'm going to get rid of it, you tell your husband. I'm going to roll it up in a sheet and drag it outside.

Leave it, your husband says. I need you to see that it won't decompose.

I won't look at it, you say.

Look all you want, he says.

To prove yourself, you roll the corpse over to your side of the bed. One of the arms winds up twisted beneath the torso—a horrifying, impossible bend in the wrist. You resist the urge to adjust. You slide over to your husband's side of the bed, across the midsection, which is a bit moist. You wish there were a stench, something to permanently disgust you, but there is only the menthol/plastic/cookie scent, which you actually don't find unpleasant.

You turn your back to the man's body and wrap your arms around your husband's chest from behind, clinging to his torso like it's a buoy. He doesn't move. You lift your shirt so he can feel the warmth of your breasts pressing into his back.

Your friends tell you to look at the body.

Give yourself permission to grieve, they say. Spend time with it, then bury the thing.

You assume the passage of a week will make looking at him easier—you will see the horrific side of death—but the corpse remains, to you, flawless. You notice some swelling in the joints, but the lips are full, the skin on the face smooth. The abdomen is a bit paunchy, but wasn't this one of the things you admired about the man, his refusal to become a slave to the gym when he hit middle age? The way he embraced his own imperfections, and yours?

You find a Christian therapist named Bobbie in the yellow pages. You choose her not because she's Christian, but because her office is in Hixson, as far from Lookout Mountain as you can get without leaving the city limits. Bobbie asks you to list ten positive and ten negative memories from your childhood. You tell her that's not why you came.

You tell her there's a watermelon in your stomach.

You tell her that every sentence you were in the habit of crafting for the other man—every thought and feeling you were accustomed to sharing—is now taking up residence inside your body.

You tell her you might just need to *unload.*

I thought you were here because you wanted to save your marriage, Bobbie says.

That too, you say.

What we find, in most cases, she says, is that the woman lacked affirmation in her childhood. We'll identify the lies from your childhood and, using various techniques such as eye movement therapies, replace them with truths.

What if the truth is I'm in love with him? you say. What if the truth is he was the one I was supposed to marry?

I assume that biblical truth is what you're most concerned with, Bobbie says.

We talked about having a baby together, you say before you walk out.

III. Active Decay: in which the greatest loss of mass occurs.
Purged fluids accumulate around the body, creating a
cadaver decomposition island (CDI).

Christmas comes and goes. The children seem happy with their gifts, but you're not sure. It's hard to listen when they speak. They are loud and clamorous with need. Your husband requires constant reassurance. The body is still on your bed, though you've covered it with a sheet, which sags over the midsection of the body, rising to a peak at the toes. You spray Febreze and keep the bedroom door locked.

On drives up and down the mountain you use the *Slow Traffic Pull Over* spaces to park the van and crawl your hands around the steering wheel, around and around, listening to yourself repeat the other man's name to hear what he used to hear, your name to remember what it was like to listen. In the shower you trail handfuls of your own hair along the wet tiles, pull clusters of it from the drain. You remember what the man on your mattress said about yanking your hair; how he knew, without your telling him, that you'd like to be handled that way.

Look in the mirror. Note the acceleration of time on your face. Smile lines have deepened; there are wrinkles beneath your eyes shaped like sideways letter "F"s.

Go into the bedroom; peek beneath the sheet. The lower jaw has fallen open. When you push the chin up to close it, a viscous black fluid oozes from the corner of the mouth. From across the room, if you squint your eyes, it looks like barbecue sauce.

You take your husband by the hand, lead him into the bedroom, show him the black fluid. You want him to feel pity for the dead man; you want him to know the man was real. Your husband punches the mirrored closet door, then holds up his fist, bloody at the knuckles. Here's what's real, he says.

When your husband goes back to work and the children are in school again, you rent a small office space. You furnish it with a futon couch and round table you find at Goodwill. In the office you reread the books you read and discussed with the other man. You watch movies on your laptop, the ones you'd talked about watching together. You make playlists. On one of them you include the MP3 of his voice reading a chapter in a Duras novel. It's the only MP3 you've kept, buried deep in a file on your laptop labeled "Vacation Pix." You spend entire mornings lying on the futon, listening to the man read the Duras chapter, a hand beneath the zipper on your jeans.

Only once do you dial his cell phone—a thrill to watch the numbers light up in this particular sequence—being careful not to press *send*.

You get up in the middle of the night to write letters to the dead man. You carry your laptop to the upstairs guest room and lock the door behind you. The letters are long, intimate, sexually detailed. The pressure inside you eases in exponential relation to the number of pages you write.

Your children knock on the guest room door.

I heard a noise, the nine-year-old daughter says, chin trembling.

I just wanted to say hi, the eight-year-old son says, shining his flashlight into your eyes.

You step out into the hallway, close the door behind you, walk them to their rooms. Lie beside them on their beds. Sing to them, tickle their backs.

You smell funny, they say.

IV. Butyric Fermentation: In this stage the body is no longer referred to as a corpse, *but a* carcass.

We have to bring it out into the open, you say to your husband. The kids can smell it on me.

There *is* no smell, your husband says.

Please, you say.

Let me do the talking, he says, removing his glasses, which have lately begun fogging up. It's been a long time since you've seen his eyes.

Make me the villain, you say.

You and your husband roll the body up in first a sheet, then a plaid quilt. You tie the ends closed with ribbon left over from Christmas. Together, you carry the quilt into the living room and lay it out on the coffee table.

The children surround the quilt. The four-year-old son yanks at the ribbon; the eight-year-old son pokes the quilt with his light saber.

No touching, you say. Only looking with your eyes.

What's in there, the nine-year-old daughter says.

It smells like when the maids come, the six-year-old daughter says.

That's Mommy's special friend, your husband says.

Why's she wrapped like candy, the oldest son asks.

Mommy's friend was a boy, your husband says.

He looks at you.

Fuck this, he says. Tell them whatever the hell you want.

You tell your children—surprise!—there are toys inside the blanket.

You tell them you forgot to let them open it on Christmas.

You tell them they'll have to wait till next Christmas.

Just think, you say—it'll be something to look forward to all year long.

V. Dry decay: Only skin, cartilage, and bones remain. If bone is exposed, the carcass will be referred to as partially skeletonized.

While your family sleeps, you cut the ribbon and unroll the plaid quilt. You will wash it and fill it with toys. You will let the children open it as soon as you're finished.

You go into the basement and find the two-person sleeping bag your husband bought for your first camping trip together. You bring the sleeping bag upstairs, pull it around the man like a pillowcase, zip it closed. You drag the man into the basement and fit the body—which you can tell has shrunk—into a broken playpen. You push the playpen into the corner with no windows, then cover the body with folding camp chairs, extension cords, leftover buckets of paint.

You arrange things in front of the playpen: a bicycle, an old armchair.

When you finish, you notice that part of the sleeping bag is still bulging through the playpen's mesh side. You kneel and run your hand lightly over the bulge, which is sharp and angular—knee, elbow.

You kiss the bulge. Lean your forehead against it. Close your eyes and imagine it's a cheekbone. You remember how the man wanted you to call him by his childhood nickname; how he said making love—real sex, if the two of you could have it—would feel like coming home.

You remember a recorded sigh, the sound of saliva on his tongue.

Your running shorts begin to sag around your hips. You pluck single gray eyebrows. You don't have the money for the microdermabrasion, dark circle treatment cream, $150 foil highlights. You buy them anyhow. You bring home wispy dresses from local boutiques; they hang in your closet, price tags dangling from sleeves.

You tell your husband you took the body to the dump and he holds you, says he's ready to make love again, undresses you slowly. He is patient with you and generous with himself. You're blessed to be with a man like this. Want him, you think. Want *him*.

You are terrified and certain that the ability to lubricate is connected to the man in the basement.

You grow desperate, watch Asian breast massage how-to videos on YouTube with links to girl-on-girl porn. You watch the porn, then call your husband and beg him to come home *right now,* telling yourself the sin of fantasy is less destructive than the sin of depriving him.

One day you click on the pop-up ads for the Jackrabbit, Silver Bullet, Astroglide for Beginners, Butterfly Kiss.

The next day you order the Classix G Natural, which arrives overnight in an unmarked box. You carry the box into your bedroom, take off the bubble wrap, and set the Classix in the center of your mattress. It arches away from you, veined and purple, suction cup at its base—a wicked, unlovely, purely useful thing.

You sit on the bed beside the Classix and whisper the dead man's name. Then you shove it back into the box and bury it deep in the communal dumpster at the end of your alley.

Come with me, you say to your husband that night. I have to show you something.

Your husband follows you down to the basement. You move the bike and armchair in the corner, then kneel, wrap your arms around the playpen, and shake it.

Listen, you say to the man. I need you to say something. Anything.

From inside the sleeping bag you hear a crackling noise, like pine straw thrown onto a fire.

Something stinks, your husband says.

Just one word, you say to the man. One of our words. So my husband can hear.

Whore, the man says, his voice muffled.

You sit back on your heels.

What the hell? your husband says.

Adulteress, the man says. *Bathsheba, Rahab.*

Your fault your fault your fault, he says.

What the hell, your husband says again.

Addict. Abuser.

He's not remembering things right, you say to your husband.

My God, your husband says, staring at the playpen. Is that him?

It's not his fault, you say. I think I just killed him too quickly.

Femme fatale.

He didn't know you, your husband says.

He puts his arm around you.

I'll take care of him tomorrow, he says.

The two of you head back upstairs.

Before you turn out the light, you turn and face the man in the playpen.

Don't worry, you say. I won't remember you like this.

LADIES AND GENTLEMEN
OF THE PAVEMENT

I'm in Start Corral Three, two corrals behind the elite runners. We're packed in tight. My bare legs are pressing into those of the men and women around me. The old man beside me, known as the Whistler, has skin the color of weathered pine. He keeps licking his lips and jumping in place.

I recognized this man as soon as I entered the corral. I read about him in *Runner's World*. His name is Jim but he's called the Whistler because of his exhale. They say you can hear him coming a quarter-mile away. The Whistler is eighty-three, and claims that before he lies down to die he's going to finish a marathon in every one of the contiguous United States, plus Puerto Rico and the U.S. Virgin Islands. Today's race—the Chickamauga Battlefield Marathon—is in Georgia, state number fifty.

The Whistler's got a pacer, a lanky teenaged boy who'll run the whole race carrying a tall stick with a sign at the top: 5-FOOT CLEARANCE, PLEASE. Also with him is a photographer from *Sports Illustrated*. She's wearing a pink singlet, her pits already sweating out. It's warm for late September. People are tossing the trash-bag jackets they gave out at registration over the corral fences. I didn't take a jacket. Who needs the friction, given our statues?

I've got mine in a backpack I bought just for this race, a moisture-wicking number with zippers and bungee cords that allow me to shift the statue around when it gets uncomfortable. I'm lucky it's so small. Some people have to wear those framed packs you see on Himalayan hikes, their statues jutting up above their heads. These runners have to be careful not to make any sudden movements. The people around them give them wide berth. It's not uncommon to see paramedics carrying away, on stretchers, runners who've been knocked unconscious by someone's oversized piece of rock.

Runners with smaller ones get assigned to the front corrals. The smaller the statue, the faster you can run.

The elite athletes' sculptures are so small they have them soldered onto rings.

You take up running. You enjoy it. You get faster. Maybe you try a few shorter races: 5K, 10K, half-marathon. Eventually, you want to run the full 26.2. And the minute you sign up, *bang*, you get a statue in the mail. You have no idea what your statue will look like, though the majority are sexual: half-human, half-animal sculptures doing lewd things with their bodies. Creatures with hideously sized phalluses. These types of statues used to shock spectators, startle other runners into a slower pace. Now they're so commonplace you feel nothing when you see them.

It's the Authentic Art that can make you lose it. A heart-breaking bend in the finger of a human hand, a ringlet of hair carved in venous gray marble. These statues are rare. I've never seen one myself, though I once saw a man lying on the pavement in front of a water stop, crying that he was devastated—*devastated*—by the white curve of a woman's breast bobbing in the pack in front of him. I watched this athlete—handsome, broad of chest, not scrawny like most runners—take off his backpack and fling it into the field beside the road. You could see why he did it: a small stone teddy bear with a crooked penis rolled out into the grass.

Such a shame, though, an athlete like that. Taking off your statue during a race disqualifies you for life. You can never get your statue back. You can never sign up for another marathon. You can quit the race, try again another time—as long as you don't take off your statue. Best to leave it on till you get to your car.

Every so often, someone claims the U.S. Postal Service lost his statue. If this happens, you sign a release and you're allowed to run with a sandbag. But you get booed by the spectators. They throw crumpled water cups at you. The volunteers handing out petroleum gel packs will toss you the reject flavors—chocolate mint, cranberry almond.

You can't choose your statue, but you do get to decide how you'll carry it. Some runners, usually beginners, prefer those front-load Snugglies left over from when they had babies. The Snuggly runners end up holding their statues against their stomachs, because of the bounce. They lose their arm-pump and look like they're going to be sick the whole race.

Besides—who wants to *see* her statue while she runs? Not me. They say your statue has nothing to do with who you are as a person, but everyone knows it has *everything* to do with who you are and what you think about. Why else would so

21

many of them be sexual? The ones who get the real art are the granolas who sit around and pluck out their sadnesses on guitars; who drive everyone else outside while they lie on frayed couches and narrate the stories of their bleeding spleens.

Sometimes your average citizens lift from bubble wrap amazing chunks of glory, hallelujah. And then they don't even run the *race*. They're just so *honored* to have received such a thing. They set their statues on windowsills and mantels and keep changing diapers or writing op-ed pieces about the manifold evils of the for-profit health care industry.

My statue used to embarrass me, but I'm okay talking about it now. I especially enjoy describing it to nonrunners, who only wish they had one. With nonrunners I can play up my statue, make it sound better than it is.

It came three years ago when I signed up for the Myrtle Beach Marathon. I'd been racing shorter distances, mostly halfs and 10-milers. You don't need a statue to run in those. But there's no respect in them. They're just *practice*. You can't call yourself a runner until you've finished a marathon with a piece of something strapped to your back.

When I lifted my statue from the box, I thought it was just a plain metal cylinder—brass, a foot long, the width of a coffee mug. Three-quarters of the way down its length, I noticed a tiny erect penis.

"What a dud," I said to my cat, who was sitting in the downstairs window of my apartment. I was standing in the parking lot beside the mailboxes, the opened carton at my feet. The breeze was lifting Styrofoam pellets from the box and blowing them around my ankles.

"Look here, cat-of-mine," I said, holding up the statue. "Is this a *joke*?"

22

The cat was fixated on the pellets. I went inside to call my parents.

"Did it come?" my mother asked.

"It did," I said.

"*Congratulations!*" she said. "Is it—artistic?"

"The folds in the *gown*," I said. "The curve of the *ankle.*"

"Roger!" she yelled to my Dad. "Pick up the other line!"

They're late on the start. Everyone has to pee. The men are whipping out their units and firing-at-will over the waist-high chain-link fence surrounding our corral. With distance runners there's a unique economy surrounding bodily functions. With a finger we close one nostril and blow snot from the other—without breaking pace—to avoid carrying tissues. I have evacuated from the back end in a number of roadside ditches, with passing traffic and not a square of toilet paper.

The corral scenario is awkward for women, though. The line gets drawn at splatter.

I end up hopping the fence and when I come back I've lost my place next to the Whistler.

At two hundred runners per corral, the total number of people running this race is around eighteen thousand. Those who cross the finish line with their statues on will have their names put into a database. Once a year, on Thanksgiving, they have a lottery: ten thousand people randomly selected to run a statue-free race in Washington, D.C.

Statue-free. These races do not exist anymore. Only the aged remember the days when we could run without a statue, or when people admitted to wishing they could run without one. Now, almost everyone is so damn proud of their pieces of stone and metal. They buy thousand-dollar custom carriers for them, run soft dust cloths over the smooth marble or steel or granite. Some people sleep with their statues, or set them up in their living rooms and tell great winding lies about the way they acquired such cunning pieces of art. They can't get away with these stories in the presence of another runner. We all know how you got your statue, bub: U.S. Priority Mail, same as the rest of us.

I push my way back to the guy holding the *Clearance* sign and wedge in beside the Whistler, who is smacking his lips. His spine is bent like a wire hanger. His statue is so small it's zipped all the way inside his Camelbak. A clear straw from the pack snakes up over his shoulder like an oxygen tube.

Before the gun, the race directors stage a military ceremony in honor of the soldiers who fought in the Battle of Chickamauga, the Confederacy's last big win. The start line is beside a grove of trees stuck through with ramrods. These trees look like acupuncture patients. Rookie soldiers forgot to remove the ramrods before firing. Each ramrod equals one dead Rebel. Some of the trees have embedded projectiles—shells, canisters, bullets. One trunk continued to grow around a canister stuck in its middle, and this tree—a three-story-high sugar maple— looks pregnant.

Now I hear the sound of drums at a slow march tempo, carnival melody on a trumpet, a piccolo feathering out trills. Beside the start line, a company of buzzed-headed soldiers in gray flannel is playing "Bonnie Blue Flag" to inspire reflection upon the Great Lost Cause. The tune does nothing to bolster the mood we're trying to create, which is Hey, hey, let's kick this road's *ass*.

After the song, the Georgia governor gets up on the elevated platform and makes a speech. He's going to run the race too. The copper statue on his back is enormous, a smiling toothless animal of some kind. The etched fur around the ears has taken on a moss-colored patina. He has to crouch to keep the ears from puncturing the canvas tarp stretched over the platform.

"Ladies and gentlemen of the pavement," he begins. "In years past, we ran without encumbrance"—he grabs onto both sides of the podium—"and this was to our detriment! We *none* of us learned perseverance. The races-of-old taught us sloth and indolence. That time is over, brothers! A new day has dawned, sisters! Today we run to prove we still know how to work, to earn our way, to persevere. We run to prove we're human!"

I don't clap or cheer. I've heard the same speech from the governors of Mississippi, South Carolina, Tennessee, and Alabama.

Just before the gun, the Whistler turns to me. "Ever finish a race?" he asks. The Whistler is bald. His pale temples appear eggshell-thin.

Here's the truth: I've tried five times. Never made it past mile eighteen. I bonk. Twice I've hallucinated and wandered off-course. But I've never taken off my statue.

"Finished seven times," I say to the Whistler. "Subfour, my last three races."

My left leg prickles against a hairy calf, while my right presses into the torpid skin of the Whistler's thigh. I think his femur would snap with an abrupt bend of my knee.

The Whistler winks. "Took me twelve races to get to mile twenty-three and figure out the secret. Now I'm just in this to win the lottery."

I've heard rumors about mile twenty-three. When I first started racing I asked other runners about it. They turned the stink eye on me. Asking for advice on finishing is poor etiquette, like letting your shadow fall across the line of a golfer's putt.

"They've upped the ante for this race," the Whistler says, lowering his voice. "That's insider info for you. Too many runners trying to beat the system. Rumor is, they're taking care of it this time. Race organizers want to send a clear message to cheaters."

Since he brought it up, I think I might ask the Whistler about the secret. But the announcer is calling the soldiers to attention. In unison, they ramrod their muskets.

"Runners, take your marks!" Musket tips lower, aim at the gray dawn just above the tree line. We freeze in the best lunge positions we can manage in our limited space. I hear the Whistler pushing air out between his teeth. Shi*you*, shi*you*. And then the muskets fire.

The early miles are a study in managed restraint. With experience, you learn to control the rush of adrenaline, run slower than you feel. The newbies are already passing the front-runners, thinking they must be some kind of athletes. Be frugal with that lamp oil, I want to tell them, it's a long night ahead.

The first two miles, you think about elbows. How to find room for yours, how to protect yourself from the jabs of others. Safest to stay beside a Snuggly runner, though I've not seen one yet this morning. Backpacks are bobbing all around me—everything from tiny pouches that fit into smalls of backs to one statue so large the guy rolled it up in sleeping bags and lashed it, with ropes, to his bare torso. There are always showcase runners like this, who make things more difficult for themselves. At the Country Music Marathon in Nashville, I saw a man running with a two-by-four across his shoulders—this in addition to a life-sized baby orangutan bobbing in his front carrier. And during the Atlanta Marathon, a woman with a bronze two-headed Weimaraner on her back pushed a double jog stroller piled high with books.

Above us the sky is slate, tinged pink just above the trees. On either side of the road are granite monuments the size of refrigerators. They're gray-white, rough-edged, with engraved metal plaques screwed onto their fronts. Behind me, the Whistler has started to emit a rhythmic *scree* sound, which—contrary to what the people interviewed for the *Runner's World* article said—is neither inspiring nor endearing. I veer off-course to check out one of the plaques and let the Whistler pass.

Pennsylvania, 77th Regiment, Veteran Infantry, 24th Brigade, 3rd Division, 70th Army Corps. A man squats behind the monument, hugging his knees and pressing his back into the stone like he wants to merge with it. The top of his head is bald and shiny with sweat. On the ground in front of him is a bulging school-sized backpack.

He looks up. "What mile is this?"

"Three," I say.

"Knew I'd never make it to five." He looks down at the backpack. "I don't think they noticed when I took it off."

"Yeah," I say, "but you might want to put it back on before they find you."

"I'm through," he says. "Didn't train. I only signed up to get *this*"—he toes the pack—"piece-of-shit flying horse. Thing's ceramic. And I'm a goddamn news anchor."

He looks up at me like he's just remembered something. "You recognize me, right? Channel Five?"

"Listen," I say, looking around to make sure no one's watching, "you want me to put it on for you?"

"Oh, God," the man says. He changes position so that he's on his knees, then lowers his face to the ground like a suppliant. The tread on his running shoes is bright blue. With one hand he beckons me to come closer. I squat beside him. "It's the wings," he whispers. "They're fucking painted."

The anchorman begins to weep.

"They'll hear you," I say; but it's too late, already a man wearing an orange *Race Staff* T-shirt is pulling up in a golf cart.

The anchorman rises to a kneel. He unzips the backpack and takes out a glossy white horse the size of a Pekinese. The rainbow stripes on the wings are uneven, the colors blurred together as if smeared on by a child. "Take it!" he yells. He throws the statue against the side of the golf cart, where it shatters. One of the wings, intact, lands in the driver's lap.

The anchorman stands. He climbs into the cart, leaving the empty backpack on the ground behind the monument.

"Never wanted to be a runner anyhow," I hear him say as they drive off. "Absolutely detest the sport."

I rejoin the race. According to my watch, I've lost three minutes, forty-two seconds.

Breathing, coughing, hacking, and spitting. The thumping of shoes on pavement. Above these sounds, birdsong. By mile four the sky has turned a pale blue and the tops of the highest trees are in sunlight. There aren't many spectators on this part of the course, but the few who are out here clap as we pass. "Keep it up!" they yell. "Keep those statues ON!"

I've settled into my pace, a solid 8:30 mile. I start to pick people off.

"He was out of shape," I hear a woman say to her friend as I pass them on mile five. "But his statue. Jesus, you almost had to bow."

"Never the athletes who get the Art anymore," her friend says. "Never the ones who deserve it."

"Whole system's corrupt," the first woman says.

People get chatty in the early miles. You don't hear much talk after mile sixteen, when the real pain starts.

At mile six I hit the first water station. Folding tables are set up in front of a battery of green howitzers. The volunteers handing out filled cups lunge toward the racers, arms stretched in front of them, backs to the mouths of the cannons. From a distance, they look like they're fleeing artillery fire.

The water stations are where quitters start to congregate, usually folks who stop running to get a drink. Their heart rates drop, they decide to sit for a minute to rest. Maybe they untie their shoes, massage their calves, strike up conversations. Eventually, large groups of dropouts are lounging all over the grass—awkwardly, with their backpacks on.

In past races I have been a lounger. Loungers stretch their hamstrings and posit questions. What are we trying to accomplish here? Do we want to run a marathon statue-free? Isn't it the statue itself that engenders the desire to run marathons in the first place? Indeed, could the euphoric—might we say, poetic—feeling in the soul of the distance runner exist *without* the statue-bearing system? Wouldn't it, in fact, be unnatural to run without one?

If not for our statues, would there be anything left to distinguish us as individuals?

A dissenter will point out the obvious: Statue-free is faster. If you ran statue-free, you would set a personal record.

To which the loungers will respond, If *that* matters to you.

A mile past the water station is a tent with a sign: *Race Counselors*. Around the tent are men and women wearing orange staff T-shirts that say *Stay In To Win!* If you feel like you want to quit, or—worse—take off your statue, the counselors are there to help. They will run alongside you and try to talk you out of it.

On mile seven a young woman in front of me—long-legged, lean, mid- twenties—is trying to wriggle out of her mesh backpack. Through the fabric I can see a blown-glass penis. It's about a foot long, transparent, really quite lovely for a standard-issue phallus. Running beside her is a counselor who seems ill-matched to this girl; he's short with stocky legs and dark hair. His torso is rotated toward her, which makes his pacing awkward. He takes two strides for every one of hers. He's holding on to her left shoulder strap.

"You're young," he's saying. "Lots of miles left on those legs."

The girl is trying to pry the counselor's hand off the left strap. The right strap is dangling off her shoulder.

"Trust me, it gets easier," the counselor says.

"You think this is hard for me?" she says. "I'm in better shape than most of these jog-bunnies. And my statue weighs, like, nothing."

"Then why quit?"

"It's just stupid," she says.

"The statues don't mean anything," he says.

"They're totally sexist," she says.

"It isn't wise to make decisions during a race. Your feelings are false indicators."

"I had my doubts long before today," she says. "Soon as I opened the box I knew what a farce this was going to be."

"It's worth it, to finish," the counselor says. "To know you're a real runner."

The girl has managed to slide the counselor's hand down onto her upper arm.

"You ever finish a marathon?" she asks.

"We're not called to race," the counselor says, his voice so low I have to speed up and run alongside them to hear. "Only to help those who are."

I glance sideways. The girl is gorgeous—blond, high cheekbones, tiny turned-up nose.

"Let go," the girl says.

"Quit, then," the counselor says, "but keep your options open."

I run a few paces ahead of them. Behind me, I hear the muted crush of her mesh bag hitting the pavement.

You hear a lot about the so-called runner's high. Before I was a runner, I figured if there was such a thing, it would hit you like an injection. You'd be jogging along and *zing*—a sudden leap into euphoria, the overwhelming desire to jump for joy and shout hallelujah. But it's not like that. It's a gradual transition into a state of mental clarity. You don't realize it's happening until you're there. For me it begins around mile eight. The smallest details become sharp. My senses open up and I can take everything in—telephone wires silhouetted against blue sky, layered bark on the trunk of a tree. The *chuk-chuk-chuk* of a woodpecker.

By mile ten I no longer feel my feet touching the ground. It's as if my mind has entered its own physical space, apart from my body, as if my body is dead but in no pain—never any pain, these middle miles. Because my body is gone, or more accurately, is on autopilot, my mind is free to roam. This separation of mind from flesh, spirit from matter, is what keeps me coming back for more, despite the fact that I keep bonking.

During the high, it's like something bigger is running *me*. If I were the sentimental type, I'd say that something is love. Because right now, mile eight, I want to tell every runner I pass how honored I feel to be a part of this fine gathering of trained athletes. I've stopped caring that my statue isn't Authentic Art. I'm convinced, if I do happen to glimpse Authentic Art rising like holy fire from someone's backpack, I won't be jealous. I'll be eager to admire and to praise. Maybe even to worship.

If only this feeling would last the whole race.

Miles nine through thirteen leave the battlefield and go through the city of Chickamauga. The town's not pretty. It's one long stretch of strip malls and gas stations, a Wal-Mart, some fast-food chains. A disconcerting number of Baptist churches. Spectators crowd the streets. Brass bands on corners play "Dixie" and "Sweet Home Alabama." Orange cones and flashing police cars block off intersections. Golf carts buzz back and forth alongside us, keeping the crowds back. Staffers speak into megaphones: *Stay behind the cones. Any assistance to runners is grounds for immediate disqualification.* Friends and family members wear brightly colored hats and hold up signs. *Lottery 2023! If You've Got Art, Show Us!*

The race organizers claim it's the hope of glimpsing Authentic Art that draws the crowds. But we all know better. Beneath the lure of aesthetic pleasure is another one: the certainty that, if you don't get a glimpse of Art, you're at least guaranteed the sight of failure—runners collapsing, ditching their statues and being hauled off in shame. As a spectator, it's best not to look into your own motives. Enjoy the spectacle, bring binoculars.

At the moment I'm not concerned about motives. I'm riding the altruism of my runner's high. The crowd shimmers and slips beside me like a river—glorious, glorious—and I see the bare kicking feet of babies in strollers, the wide milky eyes of children holding parents' hands, balloons bobbing above their heads like bright translucent marbles. My breathing comes deep and easy, the air is clear with little rifts of coolness, and I feel a melting goodwill for the men and women running around me, our hearts beating out the seconds of time.

Mile thirteen. It's getting warm out. The air has turned gauzy with humidity. I round a corner and merge onto the street that will take us back into the battlefield. Fifty yards in front of me, I see the Whistler's *Clearance* sign. I can hear his exhale. I must be running an eight-minute pace, and still I have to speed up to catch him. This guy's a miracle of endurance.

I come up alongside him and match my stride to his. The pacer is breathing hard; the photographer is gone.

"Hey, Whistler," I say.

"How you feeling?" he says.

"Fantastic," I say. My left Achilles tendon is burning and I've become hyperaware of the bottom edge of my statue jabbing into my lower back. The high is wearing off. I reach around and tighten the bungee cords.

A lemony scent is coming off the Whistler. I also smell manure and cut grass and the beachy fragrance of my own sunscreen. We're passing an open battlefield dotted with pyra-mids of cannon balls that mark the places where brigade commanders fell. Along the roadsides are markers—blue for Union, red for Confederate—placed so visitors can view the field from the vantage points of the soldiers in 1863.

"Quite an event," I say to the Whistler. "A marathon *and* a history lesson."

"Wait'll you see the Wilder Tower," he says. "Looks like a castle turret. Eighty-five feet, spectators cheering from the top."

We run together—the Whistler, his pacer, and I—for the next two miles. After a while his exhale doesn't annoy me. I begin to find its rhythm lulling. My mind weaves words around its steady tempo, little iambic nonsense phrases I repeat under my breath: *Under the spell of a linnet's wings. Gently the bell will compel as it rings.*

The Wilder Tower's at mile sixteen. I'm aware of the cheers and whistles coming from above, the Confederate flags wav-ing on the platform of the turret. But I feel like I'm reentering gravity. My legs have acquired enormous heft. Burning in my hip flexors. Pinprick tingling along my left IT band. Numbness in my soles and across the tips of my toes.

If I stop to walk, I won't start running again.

It's the statue, I think. Things would be so much easier without it.

When I used to watch golf with my dad, he would say, around the sixteenth hole, "Now we'll see how his mental game is." From this point on, finishing—just keeping my statue on—is going to be a mental game.

I once read an article about how runners can lose track of time during a marathon. A runner who finishes in five hours seems shocked it took any longer than two, while another runner, coming in at two-thirty, swears it took five.

Seventeen. Eighteen. As far as I've ever made it. But the numbers—the space and time between them—have lost their meaning. Only the words *start* and *finish* matter. Trees, fields, and monuments slide past as if I'm stationary. I reach mile nineteen, a small signpost at the roadside. One straight line, one curled over on itself. Teen*nine* teen*nine* teen*nine*. I have no idea how fast I'm going. I don't think I've slowed down. Maybe I have. I can't tell. I left the Whistler behind. He stopped at the Tower to have his picture taken.

All around me runners are beginning to stagger. I see one man take off his statue—a bronze wolf—then take the backpack off the woman beside him. She's got her mouth wide open like she's crying. The man's lips are moving. I can't hear them. A golf cart picks them up; they leave their backpacks tipped over on the street.

At mile twenty-one—twenty-one, what does it mean, I can't believe I've reached it—is another water station. A tall man with a shaved head and tarnished silver donkey strapped across his shoulders walks in circles, hands on his hips, muttering. Another man is squatting under the weight of a giant stone elf with long drooping ears, holding his head in his hands, reciting what sounds like the Pledge of Allegiance. Some runners are crawling past the water tables, their backpacks hanging off the sides of their bodies and dragging along the wet pavement. The volunteers stoop to hand them cups.

I stop running. Someone hands me a Styrofoam cup. I take a sip of red Powerade, then lean forward and vomit.

A golf cart pulls up alongside of me. "Finished?" the driver asks.

"I need a counselor," I say.

"Last tent was two miles back," the staffer says. "You'll have to make it on your own from here."

A woman in a purple cancer-survivor shirt jogs up to me. She looks fresh. "You okay?" she asks.

"Fighting," I say.

"Hang in there," she says. "Take it easy, don't push. Walk the rest of the way, if you need to."

"It's not fair," I say. "You guys shouldn't have to carry statues."

"We find that type of thinking offensive," she says.

"I'm sorry," I say.

"Just make it to twenty-three," she says. Then she reaches out and grasps my forearm. "And listen," she says. "Don't cheat. Rumor is they've changed the way they're handling it, to send a message to the running community-at-large."

"What the hell *happens* at twenty-three?" But the woman is already pressing on.

I walk a few steps. My knees aren't bending right and I can't feel my quads. I loosen the bungee cords on my backpack, shake my shoulders until the statue tips over and rests, horizontally, along the small of my back.

One shoulder strap, I think. I let the strap slide down my arm. I could take the statue off just long enough to reposition.

Behind me, I hear the *scree* of the Whistler's approach.

"Whistler," I say when he's close enough. "I have to tell you something."

The Whistler stops, hands on his hips, panting. A breeze has picked up; skinny as he is, you could almost believe the sound he's making is the wind whistling *through* him.

"I lied," I say. "I've never made it this far before."

"Figured as much," he says. His breath smells like cheese. Sweat is streaming down his cheeks and catching in his wrinkles. "Follow me."

"I can't," I say. "My legs are done. Next time I'll train with sandbags."

The Whistler turns around so that his back is to me. With one arm he reaches behind him. He unzips his Camelbak and leaves the flap open. "Take a look," he says.

I peer into his pack. Beside the clear plastic water pouch, surrounded by bubble wrap and secured with bungee cords, is a tiny statue carved from a luminous blue-white marble. It's the figure of an adolescent girl, no more than six inches tall. She's standing on tiptoe, looking into a mirror. She seems to be on the cusp of something. Her face is serene and anguished, full of ignorance and knowledge, purity and depravity. As if all of Heaven and all of Hell were condensed into six inches of stone.

"My God," I say, starting to cry. "I could spend the rest of my life looking at this."

"It's only an adjective," the Whistler says. "Points to a much bigger noun."

"How can I keep running," I say, "knowing such a thing exists? Knowing I will never earn such a thing?"

The Whistler's form is wavering like heat. I reach out to him. I'm afraid he's going to disappear. On all sides, runners are stumbling, retching, signaling for golf carts like they're hailing cabs.

"I want you to run behind me, a little to my right," the Whistler says. "Keep your eyes on my statue. We call it drafting."

It occurs to me that at this moment the Whistler is all I have.

I jog behind him. I know he's taking it slow on my account. At mile twenty-two the pacer drops his sign and we turn into the woods, moving into single file along a narrow trail—first the Whistler, then the pacer, then me. I'm grateful for the shade. Men and women in orange T-shirts line the path, standing at attention in the shadows. Patches of blue sky are visible between the dark branches and shifting leaves. I swipe at my eyes, feeling as if there is some meaning in all of this I'm failing to understand, something I've been missing all along—as if I've been running this entire race with my head turned in the wrong direction.

"There's no secret," I blurt out. "Is there?"

"Another half-mile, I think," the Whistler says to the pacer, who nods.

We come out into a sunlit clearing. In front of us, beneath a tarp tied to tree branches, a man in a dark suit sits behind a long rectangular table. He's wearing glasses. On the ground around the table and in the woods behind him—as far into the forest as I can see—are hundreds of statues. Some are standing upright; others are lying on their sides as if flung down. The clearing around me looks like a ransacked sculpture garden.

"Didn't think you'd go through with it," the man says to the Whistler. "Famous as you are."

"It's time," the Whistler says, jogging in place.

The businessman looks at me and frowns. White crumbs shiver in the corners of his lips. A half-eaten blueberry muffin, still in its wrapper, sits on the table in front of him. Beside the muffin are a stack of forms and a wire basket holding what look like fat black crayons.

"You've got two options," the man says to me, "for how you want to finish." He pushes a form and pen toward me. "Check one."

I lean over to read the words on the paper. Letters and numbers swirl.

"I can't read this," I say, pushing it back.

The man sighs. "Option one, you take off your statue and leave it here. You get your medal, your name goes into the database, you go home. You'll get a new statue in the mail."

"But I'm three miles short," I say.

"That's the point," he says. "It's a freebie."

"But I haven't earned it."

"You get over *that*," he says.

I hear spitting, panting, the sound of feet jogging in place. Runners are forming a line behind me. "Just dump your pack already," one of them says.

"How can any of us call ourselves runners," I say, "if we don't even finish?"

Above us the wind sifts through the big-leafed maples. Papers blow off the table and sway to the ground. Sunlight and shade ripple across the businessman's face. He takes off his glasses and rubs his eyes, which are puffy with dark blue dents underneath.

"Option two," the businessman says, "you swap your statue for Authentic Art and keep running to the finish. But you have to find someone willing to give up their Art." He glances at the Whistler, who's grinning. "Finish this way, you go into the database. But you have to sign, here"—he points to the form—"stating that the next time you race you'll give up your Art on behalf of another failing runner. Then you're finished for good. No more statues, no more marathons."

"What about just continuing on with what I've got?" I ask the businessman.

"You *will not finish*," he says.

"There's got to be another way."

"There isn't," he says.

"Just pick one," a woman says.

The Whistler is holding out his Camelbak, still jogging in place, knees high.

"What about the elite runners?" I ask.

"They came through hours ago," the businessman says, nodding toward a pile of tiny ivory sculptures in a basket on the table.

"So that's it?" I say. "We put in all this work, and in the end we cheat?"

"Cheaters," the businessman says, his voice low, "finish their own way."

"Just take the goddamn Art," the woman behind me says.

"The question is," the businessman says, "would you rather receive a reward for your struggles, or enjoy a reward you never expected to receive?"

The Whistler moves toward me. "Offer's good," he says. "But if I was you I'd take the first option. You're too young to sign on for Art."

The Whistler's Camelbak hangs open. Alone in her agonizing beauty, the tiny girl stands on tiptoe before the mirror.

I sprint away from the table, leaving the Whistler, the pacer, the businessman, and the other runners behind me.

The path comes out of the woods at mile twenty-four.

Collapsed runners line the sides of the pavement. Staffers are collecting backpacks and piling them into golf carts. The sun is high; it must be close to noon. The wind, really blowing now, sends empty Styrofoam cups scraping along the street, among broken glass, pieces of statue, empty gel packs, gum wrappers.

A woman in a pink cap runs up beside me. "Almost there," she says. She's wearing a small backpack. Written on her thighs and calves, in black body crayon, is the letter "A."

The woman looks down at my legs.

"You don't have a mark," she says.

"I'm doing my own thing," I say.

She drops behind me.

The fields on either side of the road are crammed with spectators. But they're no longer holding up signs or cheering. No one is clapping. The silence is profound.

Then I hear a marching band. Off-key trumpets carried by the wind, drums and oddly smeared trombones. I get a surge of adrenaline. I run past the marker at mile twenty-five. Ahead of me, in front of the crowd, I see an enormous musical outfit: fifes, drums, snares, trumpets. The crash and shimmer of the cymbals, the muted lowing of a French horn. They're playing Tchaikovsky. Playing us on to the finish!

Before I reach the band, I see something else: a twenty-yard-long vanguard of soldiers in gray, rifles at ready position.

"They've got Spencers!" someone in the crowd yells.

In front of me, a man carrying a statue—something in granite, with folded wings—collapses. The man falls backward, on top of his statue.

Then another runner goes down. And another.

None of them have "A"s on their legs.

The unmarked runners go down clean, with hardly a tremor in their bodies. The sharpshooters are masters of accuracy and calculation, compensating for the slant of the wind, the individual pace, the bounce of the stride, the precise tilt of each head.

I see a woman on the ground frozen in a lotus pose; another with her arms flung above her head, knees wrapped around the long neck of a giraffe in the posture of someone swinging from a trapeze.

Now I understand what the spectators—men, women, and children—are going to see. What they have been seeing. It's not the spectacle of failure.

What strikes me, when the bullet hits, is the absence of sound. Or maybe it's the fact that the sound of the bullet hitting its mark—the soft concave center of my temple—is a sound *like* silence. I'm stunned there isn't some kind of an explosion.

Do you see the beauty in this? I yell to the spectators as I go down. Here's your high Art, brothers and sisters! Here's your hallelujah, here's your amen!

My body is on the pavement, the music is swelling, and already I've swelled beyond it, beyond the white flash.

Spectators probably think my race is over.

But I'm pressing on to the finish. I'm surging past the crowd.

HERE

Neil Corley was driving his children to the lake cottage. He'd decided someplace familiar would be reassuring. In the back of the Suburban, all four kids wore headphones with large cushioned earpieces. They were watching *Monty Python and the Holy Grail* for the third time in four hours. They'd left the hotel in Cedar Rapids at eight that morning; Neil told his in-laws they'd arrive in time for lunch. Now he was going too fast up Iowa 71.

Had Jocelyn been sitting next to him, she would have quoted her mother: "Better 'The Corleys were late' than 'The Late Corleys.'"

A bird darted in front of the windshield, then sheared off into the corn. Stands of dark trees—windbreaks for farmhouses—rose at mile intervals from the flat yellow-green fields. The sun glinted off the rounded silver tips of silos. It was a still day in early July.

The car bucketed over a pothole. "Frozen!" Myra yelled from the third row backseat. She was thirteen.

Neil pulled the overhead screen toward the front. He glanced up—John Cleese in a chain-mail hood—the wedding massacre.

"I said to skip this scene, Grady," Neil said, pushing the *forward* button.

"It's fake blood," Grady said. He was ten; Monty Python had been his suggestion.

Neil slowed to forty-five when they entered Spencer.

"Hey, guys—it's the big chicken." He waved his arm to get their attention, and Myra pushed back an earphone. "We're in Spencer," Neil said, watching her face in the rearview. She loved spotting the landmarks. "Remember *Boy Holding Cheeseburger* at the A&W? Wake up, Effie."

In the middle row, Effie was slumped over an armrest. Myra kicked the back of her chair and Effie jerked awake. "Where we?" she said.

Ben, Effie's twin, looked out his window, then turned back. "Push *play* now?" he said.

Twenty minutes later Effie screamed. "*Giant Silver Lollipop!*"

This time the kids flung their headphones onto the floor. The Wahpeton water tower was the last landmark before the turnoff. It did look like a Tootsie Pop for a giant; Jocelyn had made up the name. Three summers back she'd asked Neil to pull over so they could take a picture in front of it. He hadn't stopped. He'd figured they'd get around to it.

The road bent, and now he could see the sliding surface of Lake Okoboji behind the houses and trees. The water was the color of lapis, spotted pewter with cloud shadow.

They pulled up to Jocelyn's parents' house. Neil's father-in-law was a retired physician; now he and Ruth were snowbirds.

Iowa in the summer, Phoenix in the winter. The Perrys' Craftsman bungalow overlooked Miller's Bay. It was shingled in slate blue with white trim work, low-slung rooflines, and a wall of French doors facing the lake.

Ruth was waiting on the front porch. Neil stayed in the car and watched the kids pile into her arms. He could tell his mother-in-law was crying when she picked up Effie. Neil smoothed his hair and looked past the house, along the grassy slope of the backyard to the trio of bur oaks at the edge of the embankment. Below the trees—though from where he sat he couldn't see them—were eight wooden steps leading to the dock and sand beach. Last summer Jocelyn and Myra had painted them to match the bungalow's shingles.

The bay was quiet: one white sail, children on a water trampoline, a WaveRunner cutting west. Over the water hung a cloud, flat and gray on its underside, rising into a crisp white peak. *Soft-serve ice cream.*

After lunch, they all walked down the street to the cottage Neil and Jocelyn bought when Grady was born. It was a tiny stone structure—620 square feet. The front door was paned in leaded glass and still had the original crystal doorknob. The toilet and shower had been installed in what used to be broom closets.

Myra and Grady unpacked and checked their room for spiders while Ruth helped the twins put on life vests and took them down to the dock.

His father-in-law opened the refrigerator and held the door wide, displaying the contents like a girl on a game show. "We bought you groceries," he said. "Just the basics." James Perry had the smooth white hair of a towheaded toddler; Neil noticed it had yellowed from the sun.

Neil looked into the refrigerator. Milk, eggs, butter, yogurt. Cheddar and sliced American cheese, sandwich meat in plastic containers, bread. Orange juice, Juicy Juice, all kinds of fruit. Condiments, jelly. On top of the refrigerator were boxes of cereal, potato chips, granola bars.

"How'd you know Naked Juice is a basic?" Myra asked him. She'd changed into a bikini with little ties at the hips. Now she was lying on the futon in the living room/kitchenette with her head propped on a pile of throw pillows, sipping from a bottle of Green Machine. What Jocelyn had started drinking when she was diagnosed.

Neil stood on the small square of linoleum in front of the refrigerator, conscious of having nothing to do with his hands.

"I'm paid to know these things," James said. "Surely you knew."

"I didn't, and don't call me Shirley," Myra said, from a movie they'd watched together.

"Did you notice the tree?" James asked Neil, closing the refrigerator. The bur oak in the small yard between their cottage and the lake had fallen that winter after an ice storm. James had the stump removed, the hole covered over with new sod, and a few feet away had planted a small emerald maple. "Give it a few years, it'll be almost as big as the old one."

"It's a really nice tree," Neil said. He wondered what they'd done with Jocelyn's hammock.

"I'm glad that tree's gone," Myra said later that night. Neil had found the hammock under the bunk beds and hung it between the shed and gazebo. Now he and his children were lying there, a jumble of naked limbs and bare feet. "We can see more of the sky."

The horizon had pinked up across the lake; behind the cottage was a silvery twilight. A slow firefly pulsed against the side of the screened gazebo.

"First star," Ben said, pointing to Venus.

"That's a planet," Grady said, but Ben's lips were already moving.

"I know what you're wishing," Effie said.

"We all know what he's wishing." Myra was sitting on the edge of the hammock, pushing it back and forth with the balls of her feet. She was sucking on a clump of her hair.

Ben opened his eyes. "I wished for a dog," he said.

"He wasted it!" Effie said. "He's supposed to wish about Mommy!"

"It wouldn't work," Myra said, standing.

"Wishing's a personal thing, Myra," Neil said, but she was already headed inside.

At bedtime, Myra sat on the counter next to the kitchen sink, shaving her legs. She'd started this in January, after the funeral.

"Why don't you do that in the shower?" Neil asked.

"Because that stall is tiny," Myra said, "and I'm a beginner. I need room for error."

He looked at Myra from behind. With her free hand she was eating from a bag of Lay's. She'd pulled her hair up into a clamp. He remembered supporting her neck, the feel of her plush newborn skull arcing backward into his palm.

Neil sat down on the couch to look at a real estate magazine. He wanted to know the going price per square foot in the area this year.

"Just once," Myra said, turning around to face him, "I'd like to open a bag, eat one, and throw the rest away." She held up the bag. "It's, like, a challenge they give you."

Grady came in from the shed holding two wooden tennis rackets and a stack of bright Frisbees. "Only two sports here, folks," he said. "One: courts around the corner, but rackets are no good. Two: Frisbees are good, but no place to throw them. No place without water."

Ben took bread and a jar of grape Smucker's out of the refrigerator and slid them up onto the counter. "I know how you make jelly," he said to Myra. "Get a jellyfish and squeeze it into a jar."

"That's right," Myra said. "That's just how you do it." Ben's head was level with the counter.

"I think it smells good in here," Effie said. She was on the floor, tapping on a small electronic keyboard. She'd said the same thing last year. The cottage smelled like natural gas and ant spray.

Me too, Eff, Jocelyn had said last summer. *When I get better let's come here, just the two of us. Let's come here and lie on the floor and sniff for hours.*

Neil stood up and began opening windows.

The summer they'd closed on the cottage, Neil and Jocelyn bought things at yard sales. They found an unopened box of silverware for a dollar, a stainless steel microwave for ten, a table and three mismatched chairs for twenty. And for no money at all, someone gave them a frayed wicker headboard, which Jocelyn spray-painted white and propped up behind their queen-sized mattress. The headboard creaked when they made love. Sometimes it bumped against the thin wall between their room and the kitchen. When Myra grew old enough to ask questions, Neil stored the headboard in the shed.

When he was certain the children were asleep, Neil went outside. A steady breeze was coming in off the lake. From across the bay he heard the churn of a Baja motor; when it faded he could hear muted laughter, the bass line of a song, and, closer, the low calls of a bullfrog. Next door someone was grilling fish.

He found the headboard in the shed behind the lawn mower, resting on its side. He pulled it out and examined it in the light of the single bulb above the door. Cobwebs breathed against the latticework. He carried it inside and wiped it with a gray kitchen rag. White paint chips flecked the towel like snowflakes on cement. Then he took it into the bedroom and slid it back into place.

That night, in their bed, Neil dreamed he made love to his wife. He dreamed he made love to her from behind, fast and aggressive. She arched into him, reached between his legs and pressed up, hard, the way she knew he liked.

When it was over, she rolled to face him, her nipples just grazing his chest. "I thought you were a stranger," she said. "It was incredibly exciting."

It wasn't the dreams, Neil thought, when he woke to the sound of a night bird in the maple, its notes a major triad sung in reverse. It wasn't even waking up alone that was so hard. It was waking up alone, for the first time, here.

"I think I killed one," Grady said the next morning. He came into the cottage and took a wide stance in front of the breakfast table, hands on his hips. He was wearing just his swim trunks. "I think I had it out of the water too long." His chin shook.

Neil went down to the dock with him. Grady pointed to a white fish struggling on its side in the shallow water beneath the dock.

"Well, that happens," Neil said.

"I couldn't find the rag," Grady said. "I was afraid I'd get cut if I didn't hold it with a rag." He started to cry.

"Hey," Neil said. He put an arm around Grady's thin shoulders. "It's just a fish."

"A stupid sheephead," Grady said. "You can't even eat them." He tossed his head so that his bangs fell over his eyes.

Neil squatted beside him to help clean up his tackle. He noticed the dirt under Grady's toenails, the scrapes on his shins, the way he turned the lures around in his fingers, fitting each one into its compartment like a puzzle piece. Grady walked up to the shed, pole over his shoulder. The tip caught in a branch of the maple, and, using more force than was necessary, he yanked it from the tree. Neil watched the torn leaves twirl and settle onto the grass.

He'd had this idea, when Myra was born, then Grady and, six years later, the twins (their miracle year, the cancer gone into remission but really only on pause, gathering itself), that he would guide them. He taught Management, Organizational Behavior, and Leadership Theory at Westminster College in Georgia. At home, he thought, he would be the CEO of his own little company. He would set directions, be there to problem-solve, be a servant-leader. And in return, they would need him. It would be enough.

But the kids seemed only to need Jocelyn—milk, comfort, the lilt of her voice. Fine—Jocelyn would need him. But over the years this hadn't turned out to be the case either. She was brilliant, beautiful, and self-contained. She came from money and love.

Neil's own father was on his fourth marriage. His mother died when he was three. He had no full-blood siblings, only half-brothers and half-sisters he didn't keep track of. Jocelyn's family, the kids, their life together, summers at the lake—he'd grown dependent on all of it. He'd created the family he never had. He was the needy one.

And when she started pulling away after the final diagnosis, having panic attacks and bouts of depression where she refused to get out of bed, he thought, *Now she'll need me.* And she did. He would bring the kids in to see her when she wanted them, take them out when she started to cry.

One evening, before he hired a part-time nanny, Neil came home from work and found Grady marching on top of the coffee table. He was singing. Ben and Effie, two years old then, were naked; Myra was sitting upright on the couch. "Where's Mommy?" he asked.

"In the bathroom," Myra said. "She said to take turns singing till you got home."

The bathroom door was locked. Neil fumbled at the doorknob with a screwdriver; then he kicked in the door.

He found Jocelyn curled in the empty bathtub. "Did you hear them out there?" she said.

The next day, she told the doctor, "My children are angels and I can't be in the same room with them."

That evening, James took them all out on the boat. Grady wanted to try his new kneeboard. "Check this out, Dad," Grady had said that afternoon, showing him the board his grandfather bought him—streaks of red and orange flames, cartoon boys with wild hair and threatening facial expressions. "No fins. I can do three-sixties on this thing."

"The guy at the marina said they're easy for kids to get up on," James said. "I thought it'd be good for him."

"It's great," Neil said. "He'll love it." The price was still on the board—$349.99.

Now they were circling Miller's Bay in the 27-foot Cobalt. WORTH THE WAKE, the back of the boat said. James drove, pulling Grady along at 20 mph. In the bow, Ruth held Effie in her lap; Ben and Myra sat in the stern. Ben was clutching the orange flag he was supposed to wave if Grady fell.

Neil stood aft, watching Grady. He'd pulled himself up right away, holding the towrope in one hand so he could fasten the Velcro strap across his thighs. He was already learning to maneuver, cutting across the wake. He dragged one hand in the water beside him, creating a line of spray.

"Cool!" Ben yelled. He was smiling. They were all smiling—his children, his in-laws.

Grady gave a thumbs up. "He says faster!" Myra yelled, and James pushed the throttle forward.

In the support group, the counselor had said: When you lose a loved one, you feel as if you're inside a confined space. Everyone else will seem to be careening along outside of this space. In time, you will become aware of an opening you are going to have to step through. It might be the touch of a new lover, a new job, a move—but you'll know. You will step through.

Neil watched Grady bounce in the wake. He felt the spray coming up from the starboard side of the boat. The scream of wind in his ears. There were things none of them knew, not even the counselor. Those last days it was his job to squirt dropper after dropper of morphine down her throat. The hospice nurses would turn away when he dosed up the medication, or leave the room—avoiding the conversation he was not permitted to begin. Jocelyn's eyes pleading with him to do what he could not. It was the last way he failed her. He filled droppers, then held her hand while she fed them to herself. He stood there while she sucked and sucked, startled by the unity of her first and last acts on earth. He held her hand until the fingertips cooled against his palm.

When the sun was low, James pulled into little Miller's Bay and anchored the boat three hundred feet out from the nature preserve. A sandbar extended into the bay and separated the lake from the preserve's wetlands. The children jumped in and walked up to the sandbar, Effie squealing about the seaweed, Ben and Grady draping green swags around their necks. Myra picked her way among the rock piles. Grady took giant steps along the section of sandbar that was invisible beneath an inch of water. "Look," he called to them. "I'm Jesus!"

"The kids are so good for us," Ruth said to Neil. "Reasons to go on living." She was kneeling on the cushioned bench in the bow, taking pictures. She was gorgeous, Neil thought. At sixty-four, her brown hair was graying only at the temples. She'd had a mini face-lift to get rid of her jowls, but she hadn't touched her eyes. "Why don't you get in with them," she said.

The darkening lake, the flock of seagulls at the end of the sandbar. The knock of swells against the hull. The children running, kicking up water, scattering gulls. They were lifting seaweed-covered rocks and spiraling them into the lake. At the far end, near the shore, Neil could see a white-haired couple paddling along in kayaks. A collie, wearing its own orange life jacket, sat up in one of the prows.

"I think I'll get something to drink," he said. He went down the steps into the small cabin. A pile of folded beach towels was on the table next to three bottles of sunscreen. He checked the galley—the wet bar was stocked. The refrigerator held Coke, Diet Pepsi, Sprite, Perrier, a six-pack of Coronas. There were juice boxes for the kids, small Lunchables snacks with ham, cheese, and crackers, a tray of sliced fruit. A plate of carrots and ranch dip.

It was dark when they got back to the cottage. Neil helped Ben and Effie pull off their wet swimsuits and told them to find their pajamas. Another yard sale purchase: the children's oak dresser, four stacked drawers with masking-tape name tags—*Myra's Madness, Grady's Getups*—in Jocelyn's faded block script. The dresser tipped if you opened more than two drawers at a time. For six summers Neil had meant to anchor it to the wall.

Now the children were fighting over who got to open which drawer first.

Neil went into the bathroom and locked the door. He sat on the closed toilet lid and tried to concentrate on his breathing, the way they'd taught Jocelyn to focus in Lamaze class.

Through the thin drywall behind the sink he could hear Effie and Ben arguing over the top bunk.

"My pillow's on it," Ben said.

"But I put books up there," Effie said.

"You'll fall out."

"Mommy said take turns!"

Neil heard the sound of books hitting the floor. He heard Myra's voice, then Grady's.

"Dad?" Myra was outside the bathroom door.

"I heard," he said. "Give me a minute."

"Did Mom say they should switch off every night?"

Neil yanked the door open. Myra jumped back, hand to her chest; Neil walked past her into the twins' bedroom.

"Ben, top bunk. Effie, bottom," he said.

"Not fair!" Effie was standing beside the dresser, wearing just her panties: the words SUMMERTIME FUN!" above a rainbow-colored beach umbrella.

Grady started picking up books. "Maybe they should rock-paper-scissors for it," he said. "Or do bubblegum-in-a-dish."

"Mommy does engine-engine-number-nine," Ben said. He was on the top bunk, looking over the rail, eyes wide.

"My tummy hurts," Effie said. She started to cry. "I want juice. I want Mommy to cut me up a banana."

Neil picked Effie up. He thought he might shake her; and then he was visualizing it, he was imagining shaking her so hard her eyes would roll, her teeth knock together. He set Effie down on the bottom bunk and held her there, gripping her upper arms. He savored the compression, the stinging sensation of the squeezing—the movement of his anger into someone else.

"Mommy isn't here," he said to her.

He let go and stood. "*I'm* the one who's here," he said, to all of them.

At midnight, Neil stood alone on the dock. The night was warm with a full yellow moon over the lake.

Across the bay, someone was lighting fireworks. He saw the flares, the sprays of dwindling white sparks. Every few seconds, there was a faint *pop*. In each small burst of light he could see boats anchored along the shoreline.

There were nights when she used to strip, jump off the dock, and swim naked in the dark water. The slick feel of her skin, when she emerged; her narrow hips, the sweep of his fingers up into her wetness; the way she coaxed him out of his clothing and, still standing, drew him inside and held him fast, his fingers tangled up in her wet hair until he exploded and lost hold of her, falling to his knees. He refused to swim, after—he wanted her smell on him till morning. On her thirtieth birthday she'd painted each wall in their tiny bedroom a different color—buttercream, wild strawberry, peach, mellow mint. "We'll be sleeping inside a smoothie," he'd said. And he remembered those unhappy evenings, after the last diagnosis, the petty arguments that came of avoiding the topic neither of them could face; the last time here, when she sat in the gazebo after the kids were in bed, thin and silent, drinking gin.

"Effie needs you." He turned; it was Myra, coming from the cottage, wearing a long white T-shirt. She was holding Effie's hand. "I took her to the bathroom and she threw up."

A corner of Effie's Barbie nightgown was tucked up into her underwear; her bangs were sweaty and she was crying. Neil walked up onto the grass and pulled the nightgown loose. He lifted her; through the thin fabric he felt the heat in her armpits.

He kissed her forehead. "You've got a fever, Eff."

"I looked for Motrin," Myra said, "but we don't have any."

"I'm sure Grandpa's got some," Neil said.

"Want me to walk down and ask?"

"That's okay, I'll go. Would you stay with Effie?"

Effie lifted her head off his shoulder. "But I want *you*."

It was only a breath, the smallest puff of hot air on his cheek. But it was there. The long hallway, the door swinging out onto the whirling planet. How strange, he thought, that his daughter's words could reveal such a thing. He felt the invisible machinery inside him stir.

Effie burrowed her face into his shoulder.

He should have jumped into the lake with his children that afternoon. He should have shown them, here, that everything was going to be okay. Tomorrow, then. Tomorrow he would pull them in, give them rides on his back. Over and over he would dive deep, come up underneath them, tickle their feet. Allow himself to be thrilled by the reach of their fingertips, the brush of their soles.

What Friends Talk About

Weekday mornings, after she takes the children to school, she drives to the local grocery and sits out on the covered second-floor balcony. This is where she goes to call the other man, though some days he calls her first. Below the balcony is a parking lot, car tops pulling in and out, train whistles from the rail line a half-mile beyond the row of Bartlett pears bordering the shopping center. In the spring, when the affair has ended, the trees will flare out in a lacy white bloom. Look at the bride trees, her youngest daughter will say, gazing through the backseat window.

In tiny print, on receipts and the insides of book covers, she makes lists of things she wants to ask or tell the other man while she sits at the table above the parking lot. She writes down things her children say—*Does the Mississippi dump into the Atlantic or Specific? When I'm at school my stuffed animals stay home and do very quiet things. Got my braces tightened today so I can only eat Pure Aid food, ugh!*—her oldest daughter's Facebook status. She tells him about her husband's trip to Singapore, the hand-strung black pearls he brought home for her birthday: thirty-seven pearls, each tinged an iridescent purple-blue.

The other man tells her about his wife, how she's training for a triathlon and got a new haircut, short and spiked. How he misses it long and silky down her back.

Don't ever cut your hair, he says.

She knows the man doesn't like it when she talks about her husband and children. He knows she doesn't like it when he talks about his wife. But these are the things friends talk about.

Later, when they've finished with talk of spouses and children and the vagaries of their daily lives, he will read poetry to her. Linda Gregg, Jack Gilbert, Sharon Olds. He'll ask her to read certain passages aloud for him, and she'll record them on the computer, then send them as MP3s. He will e-mail long passages from books on quantum physics and New Age spirituality; she will e-mail passages from C. S. Lewis and the Psalms. They'll talk about these things, too. And when they've finished with poetry and science and God, and the pauses between their sentences grow longer, she will leave the table and walk down the stairs past the sushi bar and deli and greeting cards and potted orchids near the store's entrance. She will get into her car.

Today it's raining, hard. Even at top speed the wipers can't keep up. Overnight, in Chattanooga, the rain will turn to sleet; on the mountain, where the woman lives, snow.

I'm driving home now, she says.

He draws a breath.

If our lips could touch, he says. Even once. We could be *done* with this. Put a period at the end of our sentence.

For me it would be an em dash, she says. Or the start of a new sentence.

We're going to need some kind of physical closure, he says. We need to grieve together, alone.

I couldn't be alone with you and not want everything, she says.

I'd be strong for both of us, he says. I imagine kneeling in front of you, my head in your lap. You're sitting on the edge of the mattress, I'm holding on to your belt and just—*weeping*. We'd sit at opposite ends of the room, watch each other undress, then sleep in separate beds, like twins. We'd never touch.

Back up, she says. I'm still with the belt.

The man is quiet.

Sometimes, he says, when I'm home alone, I lean my forehead against the wall and say your name.

Say it now, she says, and he does, his voice cracking on the vowel.

I can't work, he says. At night all I want is for my wife to go to bed so I can sit in my office and think about you. If someone asked me what I want right now, I would say, To go on thinking of her.

What I want, she says, is for you to make me cry, then be the one to make me stop.

Where are you right now? he asks.

Halfway up the mountain.

Pull over, he says, and she does.

Where would you want me, he says. If I could.

In my mouth, she says, and then the other. So I could walk around knowing I was carrying you in two places inside.

I don't even know what to call this, he says. It's a fucking overwhelming drug.

Addiction, the woman says, her hand moving beneath the elastic on her skirt.

61

She leans back in her seat, turns off the wipers. The passing cars blur.

Can we go into the forest? the boy asks.

He and his mother sit on one of the benches in the old amphitheater abutting the Conservatory of Music. The benches narrow down to a cement stage, behind which is a small clearing surrounded by trees—what the boy calls the forest. Sunlight does not enter the space. The trees, a dozen or so, leaf out only above the rooflines of the surrounding buildings: amphitheater in front, parking garage behind; Conservatory on the left, dormitory on the right.

The boy's mother is talking on her cell phone. It's what she does every week, now, while his sister takes her piano lesson. *I miss you*, the boy hears her say, and he feels safe. She must be talking to his father.

Can we go down there? the son asks again, pointing.

The mother looks at her watch, nods, and takes the boy's hand, but he pulls away and hops down the benches, then runs into the clearing ahead of her.

The mother finds him standing on a protruding root at the base of a four-story-high oak, its trunk striped with tiny squares of white paper. Each square, she sees, has been driven into place with a burnished nail. The squares are aligned in spiraling rows that begin fifteen feet aboveground and twist down the trunk to its base, like a strand of DNA. The mother thinks there must be a thousand pieces of paper nailed to the trunk.

The boy thinks of a giant candy cane. He rips off one of the scraps and sees writing.

Look, he says, handing it to his mother.

She turns the scrap over. "I'm sorry" is written in blue ball-point pen, the cursive delicate, the tail on the "y" rounding up in a scrolled flourish. She walks up to the tree, begins to lift the scraps to look at their undersides. Standing beneath her, the boy can see the same blue writing on each of them. He hears his mother say, *You won't believe what I'm looking at.* He hears *Some kind of installation art* and *I'll call you right back.* He watches as his mother backs away from the tree, holding her phone up.

The phone makes its camera sound.

The mother looks down to check the image. It's blurred. She takes another shot and texts it to the other man. Then she holds the scrap of paper close to the lens. She wants the man to see the writing. But when she previews this photo all she sees is her own hand, which is ugly—the part of it that shows, anyhow: thumb and index finger with chewed nails, cuticles torn, fingertips raw; the skin between crinkly, webbed. For a moment she has clarity: she is middle-aged and flattered. The man on the phone is a fiction, her own desperate creation.

She hands the scrap to her son.

Do you know what this says? she asks. Can you sound it out?

The boy shakes his head, mouth open.

I want you to keep this, she tells him. Like a present from me to you, okay?

The boy nods, clutching the piece of paper.

Okay, she says. Now hold it up, like this, so I can take a picture.

The classroom window is open despite the drizzle. Sitting in the outdoor amphitheater, the mother can hear her daughter playing a Bach Invention, low octaves in the left hand blending with a flute trilling in the classroom next door. On the floor above, a baritone voice sings a single phrase, over and over. German, she thinks. Wagner. She feels the light flutter in her stomach she used to feel before her own piano recitals. She is waiting for her phone to vibrate. Tuesday, 4 P.M.—any second the other man will call.

She looks down to where her four-year-old son is hopping from bench to bench. He's taken the hood on his raincoat off; strands of wet hair cling to his temples.

Careful, she says, it's slippery. The boy stoops to run his hands over the slick wood.

The mother turns to look at the classroom window. Inside, her daughter will be sitting at one of two Steinways, which have been placed side by side so the student can observe the teacher's hands. The teacher, Lena Ivanov, will pace behind the girl while she plays, stopping to sit down and demonstrate how strong this sforzando should be, how light that staccato. She'll ask the girl simple questions—What does the *pp* mean? How many flats in the key of F?—but her accent is strong, the diphthongs rising and falling in the wrong places, and her daughter will remain silent, staring at the calendar above the piano. It's an old calendar, from eight years ago, but Lena Ivanov still displays the months in sequence, each page depicting an important Russian landmark: the Hermitage Museum, the Volga and Neva Rivers, a statue of Pushkin.

On the way home from the Conservatory, her daughter will scowl. I don't like piano, she'll say. I don't like Miss Ivanov. But by the time they've reached the top of Lookout Mountain, she will have stopped complaining—she'll be cheerful, full of chatter—and the mother will convince herself, again, that the discipline is good for her, that it's important for her to learn to adapt to different teaching styles.

There's also the matter of the phone calls from the man, the hour of near-privacy the lessons afford. Yes, the mother will tell herself. There's that, too.

Today she'd planned to tell the man a story, something a cardiologist said about heart ablation being a search-and-destroy mission. But when the phone vibrates in the pocket of her raincoat and she hears the man's voice saying her name, she finds she's biting her lip to keep from crying.

It's like this great darkening has taken place, she hears herself say. Like I've sucked the light out of the world and into myself, and only you can access it.

It's what happens, when it's love, the man says.

I'm a sieve, she tells the man. I need more and more contact with you just to feel normal.

She looks down to where her son is pulling at weeds growing up between cracks in the concrete.

Two more months, the man says, and we'll have our meeting.

The mother watches her son toss a handful of shiny wet weeds into the air above his head. He looks up at her.

Watch this, he says, climbing the benches.

Too high, she calls to her son.

The boy doesn't look at her. He's crouching, about to leap down to the concrete stage from seven benches up.

Hold on, she says to the man.

Jonathan, she says, making her voice slow. I need your eyes.

The boy turns and, briefly, looks. She watches his body soften, the subtle, reluctant quieting of his limbs. He will not jump.

Sorry about that, she says into the phone.

The man groans.

I need your eyes, he says.

Somehow it works better than *Look at me,* she says.

The way you parent, he says. It tells me everything.

1.7 TO TENNESSEE

Eva Bock made her way along the shoulder of Lula Lake Road. She was eighty-nine—tall, bent forward from the waist. Her white pants hung from her hips so the hemlines of the legs pooled onto the tops of her tennis shoes. Her narrow lips were painted orange-red, and her steel-gray hair, tied up in a bun, smelled faintly of lemon. Loose strands hung about her cheeks and trailed down her spine. She wore a pair of headphones that created a furrow across the center pile of her hair. The cord fed into a chunky cassette deck/FM radio hooked onto the waistband of her pants. She was listening to NPR.

In her pocket was a letter, addressed: *Pres. George W. Bush, Penn. Ave., Wash. D.C.* Seven envelopes she had thrown away before she felt her handwriting passed for that of an adult. The letter itself she dictated to Quentin Jenkins, one of the McCallie boys who went down the mountain for her groceries. Quentin wrote in cursive on a college-ruled sheet of paper. She preferred he type it, and considered offering to pay him an extra dollar to do so, but when she finished her dictation and Quentin read the letter back to her, she grew excited and snatched the paper from him, folding and stuffing it into an envelope. Then she realized she hadn't signed the letter, so she had to open the envelope and borrow the boy's pen. Quentin offered to mail it for her but she had made up her mind to deliver it to the post office herself. She took great pride in the fact that she, an eighty-nine-year-old woman, still had things to say to the President of the United States. It was a formal letter, protesting the war. She felt it her duty to place it, personally, into the hands of the government.

A yellow Penske truck approached, honking. Eva set her feet a little ways apart and froze, looking straight ahead. She swayed from side to side, as if holding her balance on a log. In her freckled hand she carried a furled green umbrella, the tip of which she planted into the pavement to steady herself against the truck's tailwind.

When it passed she continued on, watching her feet take turns appearing and vanishing beneath her. One of her shoe-laces was untied. The Lookout Mountain residents never honked. She had been walking this route, mornings, for as long as she could remember. Most locals slowed and made half-circles around her so she wouldn't feel obliged to step off the pavement. The tourists would run her off the road if she did not stand her ground to remind them this was a residential suburb, where folks lived and worked and took morning walks.

Eva felt short of breath, a bit light-headed. She'd been un-able to finish her toast that morning, so eager she'd been to set off upon her errand. Three houses before the elementary school she stopped to tie her shoe. Sitting on the stone retaining wall beside the Sutherlands' driveway, she crossed her left foot over her right knee. The angle was awkward; the laces draped against her inside arch. She rested, looking up Lula Lake Road, visualizing her route. Just past the school's pillared entrance were a small pond and wooden gazebo; beyond the gazebo she could see the spire of the Methodist church, and beyond that were the bakery, City Hall, gas station, and convenience mart. Next came the Mountain Market and Bed and Breakfast. A brief stretch of houses. And then—with difficulty, Eva pictured herself reaching it—the four-way stop where Lookout Mountain, Georgia, became Lookout Mountain, Tennessee.

It was here, at the border, that Eva usually turned around, so that by the time she came home to the Adirondack rocker on her front patio, she had covered just over a mile of ground. Today would be different. The post office was on the Tennessee side, 1.7 miles from her front door. She'd had Quentin look it up on his laptop computer. Round trip: 3.4. She had not walked this far in twenty years.

She stood and, clutching the handle of her umbrella, again began her slow, measured steps. With her free hand she brushed off the backs of her pant legs and adjusted her top. She was wearing a threadbare sweater with an orange "P" knitted into the black fabric. It had been a gift from her son Thomas, who, after one semester at Princeton, joined the Army and was killed in a village in the Batangan Penninsula when he went into the jungle to relieve himself and stepped onto a booby-trapped 105 round. One arm was found hanging by its sleeve from a branch twenty feet above the ground. At least this was the story she heard coming out of her mouth when people asked about the sweater. Sometimes she forgot and said she didn't know where the sweater came from, and when she said this, it was as true as when she told the story about the dead son. She wasn't always sure if the thing had actually happened or if it was just something she read in a book. When she told the story, she felt she had not even known the boy in the jungle; she told it without emotion, as if describing a scene from a stage play, the boy who stepped onto the booby trap just an actor who was now carrying on another life somewhere.

When she finished telling the story she would berate herself. "His own mother," she would think. *What kind of mother stops feeling grief for her son? What kind of mother must I have been?* She could not remember. And there was no one left whom she could ask.

But no one talked to her about the sweater anymore. If anyone spoke to her at all, it was, "Miss Eva, why must you take your walk along this busy road? You know when the fog sets in we can't see you coming or going. Miss Eva, you're going to get yourself run over." But most people in town could not imagine what it would be like to drive along Lula Lake without watching for Miss Eva. Single-handedly, between 7:30 and 8:45 A.M., Eva Bock kept the speed limit in check.

The truth was she could no longer remember why she walked this road. "It's the way I know," she said when people asked. When she'd formed the habit, Lula Lake was not paved. Where the gas station and pharmacy stood had once been a grove of peach trees. But these were details that, most of the time, she could not recall. This morning, for example, she could think back only as far as yesterday's walk, when Phyllis Driver came out of the convenience mart and offered her a cup of Barnies coffee. She turned it down. The cup was brown with a picture of a man wearing glasses drawn in yellow lines. Phyllis was wearing a watch for people with vision trouble, large black numbers on an oversized white face. It read 8:10. Eva could remember these things—the time, watch, cup, "Barnies." She could not remember her own son.

Sometimes she did remember things, usually when the season was in a time of change, but they were memories from her childhood. When one of these memories broke over her she would laugh and clap her hands against her thighs. One October morning, she stepped into the Mountain Market, flushed and shaking. Lorna Ellis, the cashier, put out her cigarette. "Gambling!" Eva shouted. "At the college!" Except for smears of red in the corners, her lips were colorless and wet with saliva. The skin on her face was like a delicate system of roots. Miss Eva beckoned and Lorna followed her out onto the stoop. With her umbrella, Eva pointed to the ridge above the Methodist church, where the trees around the Westminster campus shone red and yellow. "That's where Granddaddy showed me how to play blackjack. Held me on his knee and taught me to add up cards."

When she did remember her son, Eva Bock prayed. It was the only time she prayed, and since she rarely remembered, she prayed infrequently. She began with the Lord's Prayer but usually wound up arguing about the funeral with Hugh, her husband, dead thirty-two years now. "Thy will be done, on earth as it is in Heaven," she would recite, imagining Thomas's soul continuing to fly upward while the rest of him fell back to earth. "And get rid of the flag," she told Hugh. "It's sullying his coffin." When they sent Thomas home in a bag with a zipper, Hugh oversaw the entire affair: the guns, flag-folding, honors from a country that served Thomas up in the name of— what? It was a question she'd asked so many times it was boiled down, the feeling refined out of it. Just a quiet string of words she wished God would tell her the answer to. Sometimes during these prayers, when she got to the part where she meant to argue about the funeral, a young Hugh Bock would appear before her, expressionless and shining in a white linen suit. He was handsome and when she saw him like this she would forget what it was she wanted to say. She would feel girlish and shy and want to adorn him in some way, perhaps slide a daisy into the buttonhole on his lapel.

Today she did not remember Hugh or her son. She thought only of hand-delivering the letter in her pocket. It was cold out, close to freezing, in fact, and her knuckles ached around the handle of the umbrella. *Should have put on my coat. But there's no sense in turning around.* She was passing the pond and gazebo beside the school. Children—looking impossibly tiny to her, dwarfed by oversized backpacks—were emerging from side streets and parked cars. They wore brightly colored rubber shoes and hats with tassels. Mothers and fathers looked at her but did not wave or say hello, which was the way Eva wanted it. It was the reason she'd started wearing the headphones. The muscles of her face no longer betrayed any expression, so that it was difficult for anyone to tell if she was feeling friendly, which she usually was not. More than anything else, while she walked, Eva Bock wanted to be left alone.

Two boys wearing hooded sweatshirts flicked thin branches over the pond like fly rods. Sunlight and shadow spotted the muddy water, the surface of which buoyed a thousand brightly colored leaves. A yellow dog sat on the bank beside the boys.

"Careful," Eva said. She had not intended to say the word aloud.

They turned to look at her. One boy laughed, then leaned over and said something to the other.

"What are you listening to?" the second boy called out. Eva kept up her wide, even steps. "Floods in Mexico," she said. "A mountain fell into the sea and the wave washed away a village in Chiapas."

The bell rang. The boys ran across the school's front lawn, the dog following, their shoes kicking up little moist tufts of grass.

Something in the way the boys ran off . . . Eva felt as if a stack of papers were shifting inside her head. *Remember*. But as soon as she tried there was only the road ahead of her, a line up of latecoming cars, children's faces like pale moons in backseat windows. Eva planted her feet and stood, waiting for the cars to pass. She listened to the British announcer reporting the collapse of a bridge in Dubai. She thought of her letter and reached into her pocket, afraid she might forget her errand and turn around at the four-way stop. She rubbed her fingers along the edge of the envelope, feeling the stamps. She'd had to lick four of them to make enough postage. Almost a half-dollar to mail a letter to the President.

She continued on, past City Hall with its wooden sign hanging by only one hook so the words *Lookout Mountain, Ga.* had to be read sideways. She passed the Fairy Bakery with its morning smells of cinnamon rolls and coffee. The bakery had opened in September and some mornings the line came out the door.

At the McFarland intersection, in front of the gas station, she had to stop to rest. There was a bench in the tiny center island, placed there by the Fairyland Garden Club. Violas had been planted around the bench and Eva accidentally crushed two of them beneath her shoe. She sat down, folding her hands around her knees. *Only a quarter-mile, Miss Eva. How are you going to make it all the way into Tennessee?* Little black spots dotted the outside edges of her vision. She swiped at them with her hand.

Coming toward her, crossing Lula Lake from Oberon Road, was the new family—the professor's wife and her two children. Eva had seen them before. They were late for school but the mother did not seem in a hurry. The boy had hair like a mushroom cap and carried a long stick. The girl's brown hair was pulled into pigtails and she wore a skirt with stockings. The mother watched the boy, who, when they reached the island, pointed the stick at Eva and pretended to fire. The mother said something and Eva pushed back an earphone.

"Sorry to interrupt. We've seen you out walking." She put her hands on the tops of the children's heads. "This is Myra and Grady. I'm Jocelyn Corley." She held out a hand. She seemed eager to be touched.

Eva took her hand and looked up. The woman had a scarf tied around her neck. *Sarkozy,* Eva heard in one ear, *like President Bush, is a teetotaler. He enjoys mountain biking. He and Bush are discussing a Franco-American holiday in honor of Lafayette.*

"We've been so charmed, seeing you out here every day," the mother said. "We even made up a limerick about it. We thought, with your permission, we could send it to the *Mountain Mirror.*"

"Let's hear it then," Eva said. She was annoyed by this distraction from her errand and by the fact that these new folks had already formed opinions about her. Again she reached to feel for the letter in her pocket. In one ear Sarkozy was speaking. *France was there for the United States at the beginning. United States was there for France during the wars in Europe. We must remind our people of this.*

The little girl stepped behind her mother, shy; but Jocelyn and the boy recited:

> "There once was a woman named Bock,
> who every day went for a walk.
> Rain or snow,
> still she would go,
> each step like the tick of a clock."

"Carrying a dirty sock," said the boy. "Looking for a cool rock."

"He comes up with alternate endings," the mother said.

"What's on your Ipod?" the girl asked. When Eva didn't answer the girl pointed to her hip.

"Oh. It's a radio." She lifted the corner of her sweater so the girl could see the cassette player. "I've got my news program on. The war."

The boy sat down on the bench and unzipped his backpack. "Are you for blue or gray?"

Eva wiped her eyes with the back of her hand. The spots were elongating, drifting toward the center of her vision.

"Watch this," said the boy, pulling something from his bag. It was a large magnolia seedpod. He turned it over in his hand. "Incoming!" he said. He plunked the seedpod down onto the bed of violas and made a crackling noise inside his mouth.

Eva removed her headphones. "Where did you learn that?"

"Since we moved here he's become obsessed with weapons," the mother said. "All this Civil War history everywhere."

For a moment Eva thought she might reach out and shake the boy by the shoulders. *In the name of what?* But then she could not remember what her question meant.

Now the mother was smiling; she was taking the children away. As they crossed McFarland the boy looked back and waved.

Eva lifted her chin and put her headphones back on.

On she went, past the Mountain Market with its green awning and smells of pipe tobacco and lard from the deep fryer, past the Garden Walk Inn with its trellised porch and dollhouse mailbox. And now began the stretch of large homes set back from the road. Two more blocks and she would reach the four-way stop. This was still familiar ground. But Eva was beginning to worry.

In the first place, she realized, now that she was near the border, she could not remember if the post office in Tennessee was actually on Lula Lake Road. She thought there might be a turn somewhere. In the second place—whether from excitement or just the anticipation of the extra length of her walk— her heart was clattering beneath her sweater like teeth in the cold. She turned off the radio, though she left the headphones on to discourage talkers. She put her hand into her pocket and rubbed the letter between her thumb and forefinger. The black spots floated up, and up, in front of her.

Past Elfin, past Robin Hood Trail. She had to stop three times to steady herself for passing cars, all of which slowed and crossed the double yellow line into the opposite lane. She saw Megan Compson wave from inside her silver van. Eva walked on, trying not to bend her knees too much. Beside the road were smears of color, red and yellow, purple and orange; twiggy bushes and small trees with dead brown leaves under them; low stone walls and white fences with latched gates. Vines with chalky periwinkle berries dragged at her sleeve and pant legs. The sun laid orange slats of light across rooftops. Dogs strolled out from porches and sniffed at her legs; the ones that barked she held off with her umbrella.

She rounded the last curve and saw the single pulsing red light above the intersection of Lula Lake and Lee Avenue. She could not remember why she was supposed to cross rather than turn around. Something about solemn duty and the government.

She reached the intersection and stood, breathing. Her lips felt dry. Beside her was a wrought-iron sign with arrows and words: LOOKOUT MOUNTAIN BIRD SANCTUARY. POINT PARK, CRAVENS HOUSE, RUBY FALLS. Another sign, shaped like a choo-choo train, read TAKE SCENIC HIGHWAY DOWN TO HISTORIC CHATTANOOGA!

Something about the government. Something about a funeral. The post office. She was going to tell President Johnson how she felt about things in North . . . She reached into her pocket and her heart rattled beneath her ribs. Surely the post office would not be in the direction of all those damned tourist traps. She turned onto Lee.

After walking thirty yards Eva realized she had made a mistake. The road curved and began to climb a hill. She had not planned on climbing any hills. She turned to go back to the intersection and the asphalt rushed up toward her. She would have fallen were it not for the umbrella, which she threw out in front of her and held on to with both hands—she had to lean back and squat to avoid falling. There was nothing for it but to continue uphill, and to do so she was forced to lean forward and bend her knees, using her umbrella like a cane. She was considerably irked by the black spots, which moved around and around in the trees on either side of her. Pinestraw blanketed the pavement beneath her; it was slippery and she moved toward the center of the road. Why wasn't she on Lula Lake Road? Why wasn't she on her way home? The sun was already above the tops of the tallest pines.

The hill became steeper; now if she stopped at all she would not be able to hold her balance. Eva made up her mind to signal the next car that drove past and request a ride back home. No, that wasn't right. She was supposed to mail a letter. She would request a ride to the post office, and then home. She removed her headphones and left them hanging in an arc about her neck.

Ahead of her was a sharp blind curve. If she didn't cross the street she might be struck by an oncoming vehicle. Eva listened for cars; hearing nothing, with slow steps she crossed to the right side of the road.

Where the pavement ended, there was a steep drop-off. Below, fifty yards down the rocky hillside, Eva could see a track. A woman was running laps. Next to the track was a baseball diamond, the grass still green. Silver bleachers gleamed on either side of the baselines; beyond the field was a playground with swings and picnic tables. The Commons, on the Tennessee/Georgia border *grass stains on his pants. The smell of leather oil and sweat. Watch this hit, I'll fly it to the moon. Crepe myrtle blossoms in a jar on the kitchen table . . .* and now a black dog was bounding up the hillside. Eva saw him for only a second before he reached her. She did not have time to steady herself. She hit at him with her umbrella, then lost her balance and fell. Her thin body hurtled down the side of the hill toward the baseball field until she struck the trunk of a maple tree with her left hip bone.

She lay on her side among rocks and fallen leaves. For a space of time—seconds? hours?—she thought she had finished with her walk and was now resting in her own bed, and for this she felt an overwhelming gratitude. Interrupting her sleep was a dog's bark, abrupt like the scrape of a chair being pushed back from a table. A leaf blower droned, a bird sang. The sifting of leaves, then a quick panting, very close to her ear.

She opened her eyes. The black dog was in front of her; she saw his paws, toes spread on the uneven rocky hillside, cluster of silver tags hanging from a purple collar. He barked and Eva threw an arm over the ear that was facing upward.

The sleeve of her sweater was torn and pocked with hitch-hiker burrs. She noticed her earphones were gone. The dog stopped barking and began to sniff around her face. Warm tongue on her cheek. The dog whimpered and backed away, then disappeared down the hillside.

The trunk before her was twisted about with a vine of bright pink leaves. In her confusion, Eva thought they were hands clamoring to reach the top branches, each leaf five fingers pressing into the bark, staking its claim. She rolled her head and saw that the vine ended halfway up the trunk; at the top of the tree the branches were thin and white, with only a few yellow leaves still attached. Through the branches the sky was an exhilarating blue.

She remembered: She was going to the post office in Tennessee. She was going to deliver a letter to President Bush.

What foolishness! She should never have attempted such a thing. Twenty years she had stood up to speeding tourists, and all anyone would remember was that she had fallen off the side of the road because of a dog. And what did she know about the war? Listening to NPR had only given her ideas, had made her forget who she was. She was an eighty-nine-year-old pacifist who could not find her way to the post office. Who could not remember her own son.

What do you know about the decisions of our government? It was Hugh's voice. He was standing in the driveway next to her; in her hand was the garden hose.

I know our son is dead. Cheated out of his birthright by his own country. I know the President is a liar.

Hugh slapped her across the face. She stumbled backward into the hydrangea bush. *Your son died in the name of this country. And here you are, setting your goddamn table with goddamn linen napkins.* She lay in the bush, looking up at the sky.

But something was not right with the sky. The black spots had returned and now swirled in front of the blue and branches and the yellow dangling leaves. Eva let her head roll back so she was again looking at the vine on the tree trunk and the black spots came with her, they went out to join the leaves, or the leaves peeled off and joined the spots, she couldn't tell. They were coming together, the colors merging into a subdued gray, approaching her, arranging themselves in a dark processional.

In her mind, Eva righted herself to meet them.

The spots drifting toward her were soldiers in uniform. They were all identical—all her son. She cried out and tried to touch one of them but the sons did not look at her as they came on. As they neared, Eva saw Thomas's face over and over again—his high cheekbones; the slight depression across the bridge of his nose, left there when he broke it against the handlebars of his two-wheel bicycle; the scar below the downy blond arch of his right eyebrow; the cowlick at the center of his part above his forehead. She used to wet down the cowlick Sunday mornings before church. His hair was soft and during the sermons she twirled it through her fingertips.

The faces came on. She could see the green and gold of Thomas's eyes. None of them saw her. The sons drifted past and out of her vision in a regular, stolid rhythm.

"Look at me," she said. "I want to ask you a question."

One of them stopped and turned his head. His face remained expressionless and the others waited patiently behind. She understood that he was waiting for her to ask the question and it was terrible, this passionless waiting man who was her son, terrible that he did not recognize her. She felt certain that, were she able to kiss his cheek, she would remember how to feel sadness and grief, love and longing.

In his gray uniform the son continued to wait. Eva could bear it no longer. "In the name of *what?*" she cried out to the son in front of her. "*Of what?*" she asked the waiting ones behind him. The son smiled and for a moment Eva thought he would comfort her. She saw his lips move but no sound came out. The others smiled in exactly the same way as the first.

And then they were pulling back, all of them, one by one. With horror she realized they were leaving her and she felt at the very least she should say something to put Thomas at rest. But the sons were not at rest—they were only apart, winnowed from victories and failures. While she watched they withdrew into the sky, grown dark now. They began to circle above her with a hard, impartial energy, like the stars.

Now the dark sky and circling soldiers started to descend and she understood that the darkness would cover her like a hood. Eva saw the last gray soldier turn. This time it was Hugh Bock's face before her and when he spoke it was only a whisper.

"Unanswerable," he said. And the host of orbiting sons repeated the word until it became a kind of song, the sound of air moving in summer trees: *Unanswerable, unanswerable.* Beneath them, Eva listened.

The dog was, in fact, a female retriever named Pearl. Her barking alerted her owner, Sharon Miller, who was running laps on the track at the Commons. Pearl led her up the hillside to Eva Bock's body, her leg wrapped around the trunk of a tree. One of her shoes was missing and her thin foot in its dirty white stocking looked like a child's. Her hair was spread out across the rocks and colored leaves in a way that would have been almost sensual had she been merely asleep. Her eyes were open, wide and antique, and there was a vertical gash shaped like a parallelogram from her temple to her jaw. The frail skin looked as if it had been freshly shucked. Sharon Miller could see the grayish skullbone. She vomited, then called 911 and the Lookout Mountain, Georgia City Hall. She also called her husband, who called Liza at the *Mountain Mirror.* Assuming Miss Eva had been, as long predicted, run off the road by a tourist, Liza posted the information on the *Mountain Mirror*'s website, so that, for a time after her death, the Lookout Mountain residents felt a sense of indignation at the license plates from anywhere but Georgia or Tennessee.

Because she had fallen on the Tennessee side, the ambulance came not from the Walker County, Georgia, response unit six miles away, but from St. Elmo at the base of the mountain. It took seventeen minutes, during which time residents gathered and peered down the side of the hill. Dr. Bailey was called—he was young and took the steep hillside with ease—and was able to determine that Miss Eva was, indeed, dead. Just the same,

he administered CPR until the EMTs came. Everyone felt it
was a heroic gesture.

Before the night-shift CNA at Memorial Hospital threw out
the white pants—bloody at the knees, both pant legs cut off
the victim from the hemline up through the waistband—he
found the envelope in the pocket. He was an immigrant from
Haiti, nineteen years old, and had never seen 15-cent stamps.
He felt this must be an important letter; he was surprised the
EMTs had not removed it from the pocket for the next-of-kin.
He could not read the words on the front but he opened the
letter to see if there was any money inside. Then, feeling guilty
and superstitious, he went into the supply closet and resealed
the envelope with Scotch tape.

When he clocked out the next morning, the CNA gave the
letter to the woman who volunteered at the front desk, who
placed it in a stack of outgoing mail.

Seven months after Eva Bock's funeral (during which the local
police closed 58 South to tourists, to ensure that the funeral
procession could head down to the cemetery in St. Elmo un-
impeded; the residents, who had already simplified Miss Eva
the way the living do, felt it was her final triumph), a letter in
an eight-by-ten white linen stock envelope, addressed to Mrs.
Eva Bock, arrived at the Lookout Mountain Post Office. Steven Ruske, Receiving, had never seen a letter from the White
House. He was supposed to shred it (there was no next-of-kin
listed on the Bock account) but who would know?

On his lunch break, despite the fact that it was a felony—
didn't he, of all people, know it!—Steven Ruske took the letter
out to his car, which was parked on Lula Lake Road across

from the post office. He opened the envelope beneath his steering wheel. It was only a form letter with a stamped signature. He read it anyhow.

Dear Mrs. Eva Bock,

Thank you for writing to express your concerns regarding our efforts to improve the lives of the Iraqi people. I want to assure you, personally, that I and my administration are doing everything within our power to minimize casualties, both military and civilian. Please continue to keep our troops in your thoughts and prayers as we look forward to a future in which the freedoms we enjoy as Americans—including the freedom of speech, which allows citizens like yourself to speak out against oppression and injustice—are made available to our fellow citizens at the far reaches of the globe.

Sincerely,

President George W. Bush

Steven Ruske slid the letter back into the envelope. He finished eating his sandwich, placing the letter in his lap to catch the crumbs. He stuffed the leftover crusts, foil wrapper, and envelope into his brown lunch sack. Then he crossed the street and, before returning to work, tossed the sack into the dumpster next to the Lookout Mountain Café.

THE ANOINTING

Seven months into her husband's depression, Diane called the church secretary. She wanted the elders to come over and anoint Mitch with oil. He hadn't put his pants on in a month. In the past week he hadn't left the bed. When he spoke, it was about endings—the end of his career, the end of suffering. This morning, at 3 A.M., he'd woken her to ask if summer was over yet. It was early June. Diane was afraid he might kill himself.

She'd seen anointings performed twice before. The first time was at a Baptist summer camp when she was nine. During evening worship—held in a makeshift auditorium beneath a stained canvas tarp—a boy with braces on his legs was brought forward by his mother, his wheelchair leaving tracks in the sawdust. The camp's pastor removed the braces, knelt in front of the chair, and rubbed oil all over the boy's white calves as if he were applying sunscreen. The following summer the boy came back to camp still wearing the braces, though now he used crutches with metal cuffs around the wrists.

The second time was last year in church, during Sunday morning service. A woman with breast cancer—metastasized—knelt beside the altar while the elders crowded around her, their hands on her shoulders. Pastor Murray oiled a thumbprint on the woman's forehead and prayed that God would "strangle the tumors." Now, a year later, the woman was cancer-free. She wore her hair gelled up into bleached spikes.

Anointings were eleventh-hour efforts—what you asked for after you'd asked for everything else. Had someone ever told her she'd be asking for one, Diane would have laughed. Three years ago Mitch's orthopedic practice was bringing in more money than either of them had anticipated. He'd been working long hours, not only seeing patients in the office and doing hospital rotation, but also testifying as an expert witness in lawsuits. "These guys'll try anything to get workmen's comp," he'd said. "One guy rolled himself into the office in a wheelchair. Two days later surveillance caught him pitching a tent at his son's scout camp."

Now Mitch was the one applying for permanent disability. Simple brain chemistry, the psychiatrist had said. Dopamine highs, serotonin lows. Mitch was—here the doctor had cleared his throat—bipolar. He'd pronounced it gently, as if the word itself might break in two. For one crazy moment Diane thought it meant Mitch needed glasses, the kind you wore if you were both near- and farsighted.

What it meant, in practical terms, was that for three years Mitch had been addicted to Vicodin. He'd gotten hooked after his back surgery, started mixing it with Valium and prescribing to himself using other men's names. Diane had seen the bottles on his desk—Glen Sanderson, Brian Gilbert, Gary Dennis—names of patients at the homeless shelter where they both volunteered through church. Crossroads, it was called: the logo was a cross casting a purple shadow onto a stick figure lying prostrate in the middle of a road. It was their family's ministry. Every other Saturday they drove to the facility in downtown Tucson, where Mitch handed out medications, Diane scrambled eggs or flipped pancakes, and Ellie and Kyle passed out Ziploc baggies filled with miniature bottles of mouthwash, antibacterial hand gel, deodorant, plastic combs, dental floss, tracts. The homeless people loved to touch the children's faces and hair. Diane always watched to make sure the touching was appropriate.

Then one day last November, when Mitch left early to pick up some prescriptions before work and she'd seen the kids onto the bus, the doorbell rang. Two men wearing Polo shirts and khakis held up badges. Diane led them into the living room and sat down on the couch; the men remained standing. One took out a recorder and placed it on the grand piano. "Mrs. Stewart, are you aware that your husband has been prescribing himself narcotics? Are you aware he's been using other names to obtain the medications?"

She shook her head. "He took them once," she said, "only for a few days. After his back surgery." The men looked at each other. Diane lifted her chin. "He volunteers at Crossroads, downtown. The medications are for the patients."

The DEA fined Mitch $25,000. The medical board sentenced him to a monthlong inpatient detox program and three years' attendance at NA meetings. They revoked his license to prescribe narcotics and set him up for psychiatric evaluation. "At least he didn't have to go to prison," the psychiatrist said to Diane.

Mitch withdrew from her, from the kids. He wandered around the house in his boxers. He watched the History Channel, sometimes all night long. Diane started sleeping in the guest room. She called the prayer hotline at church; she memorized scripture and took prayer walks; she went to the church and had elders pray with her. At first she begged God to heal Mitch. Now she just wanted God to extend a measured grace—something long enough to get them from *here* to *there*.

Diane wanted to believe the anointing would be that thing. But she doubted it would work. Her faith was waning. What if it was all a crock, made up to quiet fears of not existing? Near-death experiences, angelic visitations, visions—all just neurons firing, a highly evolved response system to keep the human race from going insane?

She'd made the choice to believe when she was a child living in Toledo. One winter night, when she was nine, she couldn't sleep, sweaty and panicked by the thought that she might not believe in God. She finally sneaked out of the house and wrote in the snow with her finger, in the biggest letters she could make, "I LOVE GOD." The snow sparkled orange under the streetlamp. *He can see that,* she thought. *I love Him. Now He knows.*

Lately she was questioning everything. *Maybe Hume was right,* she thought. *We should be no more afraid of ceasing to exist after we die than we're afraid we didn't exist before we were born.*

Ellie shuffled into the kitchen wearing a T-shirt Mitch had given her for her eighth birthday: a silkscreened kitten above the words LESS PURR, MORE GRRR. "What's for breakfast?"

"Pancakes," Diane said. "From scratch."

"Can you make them chocolate chip?"

"We don't have any chocolate chips."

"We never have *anything* anymore." Ellie said. "Why can't you go to the store? Or why can't Daddy?" She sat down with her knees up, her arms crossed over her chest.

"Grandma's coming the day after tomorrow." Diane knew the singsongy voice in which she said this was overcompensation. "So I can go to the store then." She poured one and a half cups of milk into the flour mixture, cracked two eggs into the bowl, and tipped four tablespoons of canola oil over the side. She stirred with a fork, then poured three circles of the batter onto the griddle in the shape of Mickey Mouse's head. She watched the face and ears bubble up and pop.

After breakfast Diane turned on Playhouse Disney. "Can I plug it in?" Kyle asked.

"Not *that* again," Ellie said to him. Kyle was six and loved anything with a plug. At bedtime a few weeks earlier, he told Diane he'd decided what he wanted to be when he grew up: a plug man. "You know," he said. "The guy who goes around to people's houses and plugs stuff in for them." She told Mitch about it later that night. Mitch rubbed the palms of his hands up and down along the recliner's leather armrests. "I'm sorry," he finally said. "What was it he did?"

Diane turned off the cable and watched Kyle pull the plug, then reinsert it. "Big to big, little to little," he said. "That's what plug mans know how to do."

Diane took Mitch's pills and a glass of juice into the bedroom. Some days she longed to curl up naked against him; other days she dreaded even looking at him. He'd aged. He was thirty-eight but looked a decade older.

Diane pulled back the curtains; Mitch stirred. She sat on the edge of the bed next to him. As usual, he held a pillow over his head. She'd hardly seen his face all week.

"I made pancakes." She put her hand on his back. "Don't you want to get up and put your pants on?"

Mitch turned over and lifted a corner of the pillow. Red lines ran in haphazard cross-stitch from his cheekbone down into stubble. He smelled musty. She handed him the glass of juice and he reached for it, his hand shaking.

"What time is it?" he asked.

"Almost nine." A cicada rasped in the mesquite tree outside the window. "Pastor Murray is coming today," she said. "He's bringing the elders. They want to anoint you with oil." She pulled the pillow off his head.

Mitch flung an arm over his eyes, then sat up on his elbows. "Do the kids still think it's my back?"

Diane nodded. She walked to the closet and pulled a pair of khakis off a hanger, then folded the pants and placed them on the foot of the bed.

Mitch lay back down. "God, I want this to end."

Diane pulled off her nightgown and stood in front of him, naked. Her breasts ached to be touched. "Then get out of bed and put your pants on," she said.

"Come on in," Diane said when the pastor and elders arrived. "Mitch is expecting you." She thought they'd have a small vial, like a test tube—maybe something crystal—but Pastor Murray stepped in carrying a family-sized bottle of Wesson Oil. Diane was startled, not just by the oil (would something from Sam's Club *work*?), but by the image of Florence Henderson that popped into her head, wearing padded mittens and frying up a mess of chicken.

The elders followed her to the bedroom. There were five of them, plus Pastor Murray. "I'm not sure he's awake," Diane said.

"Don't worry, I've seen this done for people in comas," one of the elders said.

Mitch was lying in the same position, pillow over his head. Diane sat beside him. The elders gathered at the foot of the bed.

Mitch pulled the pillow away and looked down at the elders, then at Diane. His eyes were bloodshot.

Pastor Murray came around to stand beside Mitch. He was still holding the Wesson. "We're here to pray for you, Mitch. If you'll have us. Anoint you with oil in the name of the Lord. 'And the prayer offered in faith will make the sick person well'— that's James, chapter five."

Mitch cleared his throat. "This is embarrassing," he said.

"We'd like to lay hands on you, if that's okay." The elders were coming around to stand with Pastor Murray; one of them sat on the edge of the bed.

"Sure," Mitch said. "But no funny business, guys."

In seven months, it was the first time Diane had heard him make light of anything. She knew it was for the benefit of the elders. Why couldn't he make the effort with her?

"I'll leave you men to it," she said.

"You're welcome to stay," Pastor Murray said.

"I need to check on the kids," she said, heading toward the door.

"Lord, we lift this man up to you," one of the elders began. "We acknowledge you as the Great Physician."

Diane closed the door behind her.

When the anointing was over, Diane walked Pastor Murray out to his car. "Depression's a murky thing," he was saying. He opened the rear door and set the bottle of oil on the floor;

91

she noticed that he was wearing his deceased wife's wedding band pushed up onto his necktie like a napkin ring. "A lot of Christians think it's a spiritual problem, with a spiritual fix. But it's deeply connected with physical causes."

"It *feels* spiritual," Diane said. Sweat darkened the front of Pastor Murray's shirt.

"There's heredity, for one thing. Distressing circumstances. Various illnesses that weaken the mind's ability to cope."

"Don't you think he seems worse? He's not even getting out of bed."

Pastor Murray put a hand on her shoulder. "Seasons of darkness are normal in the Christian life, too. Bunyan, Carlyle, Cowper—even Spurgeon suffered from depression. Because of his gout."

"Looking back there were signs," Diane said. "He was working too much, spending too much money. But I never thought he'd end up like *this*."

"He hasn't ended up." Pastor Murray reached into his pants pocket, pulled out a bandanna, and wiped the sweat off of his forehead.

"I don't feel like praying anymore," Diane said.

He folded the rag and put it back in his pocket. "Nothing depends on your feelings." He got into his car, then leaned out the window and took her hand. "You should go talk to him now. And remember: God holds us, even when we have no strength left to hold Him."

Diane went back inside. Ellie and Kyle were still watching Playhouse Disney in the family room. It was after eleven; they'd been watching since eight-thirty. She needed to get out of the house for a while. Their father was right down the hall. Let him be a father.

She walked to the end of the driveway, turned, and started up the gradual incline to the top of their street. It was at least a hundred degrees already. At the top of the street she had to sit down. She folded, pretzel style, onto the steaming asphalt next to an armless saguaro. She felt the sun on her shoulders and knew that freckled red patches were forming on either side of the straps of her tank top. There was something godless about the desert. General revelation didn't apply here. The notion that even if you'd never heard of God you could intuit something of Him through nature—it didn't work in this wilderness of succulents. Only the Native Americans had learned how to bend the plants to human use, fashioning the ribs of dead saguaros into spears so they could reach up and slice off the fruits. Maybe that was the revelation of the desert: God helps those who help themselves. Well, hadn't she done that?

She stood up, brushing off the back of her jeans. She would choose to believe the anointing had worked. That there would be some change. That she and Mitch would embrace and begin the path toward healing. God would never give her more than she could handle. It said that in the Bible. Nothing beyond what you can bear. She and Mitch were only being tested, refined like silver.

When she came back into the house, Diane didn't know what to expect: Mitch sitting up, his body slick with oil? Or just getting out of the shower? Or standing in the bathroom, already showered, putting his khakis on?

But he was still under the covers. His head was under the pillow. It looked like he'd never moved.

She yanked the pillow off and looked for the oil. Mitch reached for the pillow on her side of the bed, but she pulled

off the comforter and looked him up and down—the white
boxers, wrinkled T-shirt. "Where'd they put it?"

Mitch didn't move. She dragged her fingers through his
hair, but felt no oily patches.

"Please look at me." Mitch half-opened his eyes. "Where
did they anoint you with the oil?"

"Not sure," he said. "Forehead maybe?"

"Didn't you feel it?"

"I took a Valium. I've been taking them for a while."

It had all been confiscated: the DEA had gone through
every drawer. "Where'd you get Valium?" Mitch closed his
eyes and rolled over.

Diane pulled him back and he covered his face with his
hands. "Ellie," he said. "It's not her fault—she has no idea
what they are."

The room tilted; Diane's head prickled as if tiny shards of
glass were lodged in her brain.

She found Ellie lying on her bed, reading a book. Ellie glanced
up, then shrank back against her pillow.

Diane felt short of breath and placed a hand on the door-
frame. "Ellie." Her voice had plunged an octave. "Show me
where those pills are."

Ellie's eyes widened. Still holding the book, she got up
and went to her dresser. She laid the book down, opened
one of the drawers, and pulled out a small felt purse. Mitch
had brought it home for her after one of his conferences. It
was purple, with iridescent sequined flowers stitched across
the front. Ellie took it to church every Sunday. Diane always
looked inside to make sure Ellie had a dollar bill to put in
the collection plate.

She opened the snap and rooted around: a lip gloss with no lid, loose change, a tiny notebook, three broken crayons.

"You have to open the zipper," Ellie said. She got back on the bed.

Diane saw a tiny zipper on the outside of the purse, just underneath a large daisy. How had she never noticed it before? And there they were: a couple of dozen small round pills, scored across their middles. Most were blue; a few were yellow and white. They could have been Smarties, pastel Skittles, Easter-themed M&M's. "When did Daddy give you these?"

"They're vitamins to help his back get better."

"Why didn't you tell me?"

"We were going to surprise you. When he got better."

Diane bent down so they were eye-to-eye. "Ellie, it's very important for you to tell me something. Did you ever eat any of these?"

"Daddy said promise not to."

Diane stood up. "When do you give them to Daddy?"

"Just sometimes. When he's watching TV."

"What about today? When did you go to him?"

"When you were outside. Me and Kyle just wanted to see him."

"Kyle was with you? Does Kyle know about the pills?"

"It was only me and Daddy's secret."

"How many pills did you give him, Ellie? When you went in?"

"Just a blue one."

Diane sat on the bed next to her and put an arm around her shoulders. "Do you know why Daddy takes these?"

"Because he wants his back to get better. And you won't let him take his medicine."

"He takes them because he's sick somewhere in his brain," Diane said. "He's not allowed to be a doctor anymore."

Ellie got off the bed and backed away from her. "He just has a bad back. You even said so." Her chin was shaking. "I don't care if he's a doctor. He's still Daddy, and you won't even let us *see* him."

All the forced smiles, the playdates and TV programs to keep them busy, the chipper half-truths. "I didn't want to upset you and Kyle," she said. "But you have to believe me."

"I believe Daddy." She turned and ran out the door.

Diane turned the purse over and let the pills fall into her palm. She selected a yellow tablet and placed it on her tongue. Its sweet coating turned slick in her mouth, but once the surface melted away it tasted like burnt chalk. She spit it out into her hand.

As she walked toward their bedroom, she felt as if her body were stationary, the rooms and hallways sliding past. The door was open, the room filled with light, and she saw her husband and children, all on the bed together. Ellie was curled into the arc of Mitch's chest and legs; his chin rested against the top of her head. Kyle lay on his side behind them, one small arm flung over Mitch's waist. Mitch said something into Ellie's ear and she laughed, not her girlish giggle but deeper. A woman's laugh.

Diane felt something, like a hand, pressing on the top of her head, as if forcing her down to a posture of humility. She sank to her knees in the doorway. "I love you," she whispered, not to any one of them in particular, but to all of them: a triptych, a sacred tableau. She would do anything to save them.

Kyle sat up. "Mom," he said. "Come here."

Yes, she thought. *That's it. I need to get onto the bed.* But something was pressing her lower, onto her face. She fought for a moment against her rising panic, then let herself sink. She heard Kyle say something else but she couldn't make it out. She tried to lift her head, but her face pressed into the carpet. She would do anything to save them; there was nothing she could do to save herself.

IMPERFECTIONS

I want you to meet my wife, he said. We need to tether this—whatever this is—to the *space-time continuum*.

I saw their dog first, a yellow Lab mince-stepping from the hatchback, each paw shaking on the upstep, old. His wife emerged from the driver's side and kicked off her flip-flops. He doesn't do well on long drives, she said, smiling, but when I reached out to shake her hand she was already turning back to the car, gathering trash. I scratched the dog's head while he peed on the curb.

The man looked at me. I was going to sign your copy, he said, so I invited him and his wife to come up to the now-empty hotel room, where one of his lithographs was packed in my bag. His wife said, I'd better stay with Hank. And then I said the important thing, the thing I hope he remembers: Oh, then I'll just go grab it.

No, he said. I'll come up with you, and barely out of her sight the man put his arm around my waist, whispered, You're perfect, took my hand, and pulled me upstairs where my luggage sat just inside the door; and what I want to say, here, is that he threw me onto the mattress, but the truth is I sat stiffly on its edge while he signed the print, then handed it to me. *All the things I can't say*, he'd written, and then he was—not cupping, not cradling, but *palming* my cheeks, hands flat, like he was about to pray.

I closed my eyes. *After seventeen years of marriage*, I thought, *someone else is going to*—but he kissed my forehead, a long press, one Mississippi two Mississippi three Mississippi, until I said, too loud, Go be with your wife, because it was the only thing to say, and his lips were *that close*, and somewhere a voice said *Joseph and Potiphar's wife—flee*.

The kiss made my right eye burn. After he left I flushed it with cold water but the burning grew unbearable, so that during the two-hour shuttle ride to the airport I had to keep both eyes closed. *Like you put a seal on my forehead*, I wrote to him later, *and hot wax dripped down into my eye*. I kept rubbing it, kept pressing my face hard into the backseat window, my headphones on, listening to the playlist he'd made for me the night before while we sat on his bed with our laptops open and saw pictures of his wife, their trip to Prague, Hank jumping off a diving board; pictures of my husband's birthday, the boys spray-painting the number 40 on the garage door, the girls giving him the "40 Reasons We Love You" poster they'd made. What we were saying without saying it: *Here's why this can't happen*—what we would keep saying during the following months of Just one last breath before we hang up, let me hear you say my name, your name, any name, won't you please send me a picture of your foot, breast, ear, some part of you so long as it's you; and when I said, Well, but there are freckles, plus this funky trilobite mole just above my navel, he said—another thing I hope he remembers—But it's your imperfections I want to fuck.

100

You Look Like Jesus

I didn't keep the photographs he sent. At the time, deleting them felt like a way to *esteem* my husband.

I remember the important ones. A cell phone picture he took during a long run: waist-up, eyes squinting, face shining with sweat. Rows of white tombstones behind.

Here I am, his text said. Please call.

You're a beautiful man, I said when he answered.

You have no idea how much I needed to hear that, he said.

Another one: he was sitting on the floor, stretching, legs long in front of him, feet bare.

People tell me I have nice feet, he said.

I looked, zoomed in, looked again.

They're shaped like mine, I said.

Show me, he said.

I took my shoes off and angled the computer down, clicked the red camera.

That confirms it, he said. We're related. From the same soul-cluster.

I want to show you more, I said.

He was silent. Then: So far, we haven't done anything we couldn't tell our spouses about.

I know, I said.

Ten seconds, he said. I'll look for ten seconds and delete.

I took my laptop into the bedroom and locked the door, undressed and got up on the bed, lying on my side. The sheer curtains over the window behind me gave my body—cropped neck to mid-thigh on the screen—a backlit luminosity. Just before I took the picture, I slid one hand down, between my closed legs, so that my upper arm pressed my breasts together, my hand covering the bit of blond-brown hair.

I sent the picture to my husband first. *New wallpaper,* I wrote in the subject line. Then I called the other man. I heard the e-mail ding on his end, the sharp intake of his breath.

It's the curve of your hip, he said. The concavity of your navel. You're thin, but cut like a woman.

Thank you, I said, disappointed that he didn't say anything about my breasts.

Oh, I could go on—the photo where he was holding a football with some famous player's signature but all I could look at were his fingers, long and square, imagine what they would feel like inside me, on the upsweep; his nephews at Central Park Zoo, their windblown scarves, both of them fair-haired like their uncle; the scanned image of a page from his elementary handwriting workbook, *The angels worship Jesus* written over and over, parochial school cursive loosening down the page.

And the one I never told my husband about.

What did I look like to you, before we met? he asked me on the phone. The night of the opening, when I kept staring?

Focused, I said. Like you had a question and knew I had the answer.

Check your e-mail, he said.

He'd taken a picture of himself at that very moment: leaning way back in his office chair, reclined almost flat, clothes off, eyes closed. One hand was holding the phone to his ear, the other arm flung out to the side. His mouth was open slightly, his brow furrowed as if in pain. An erection arched rose-colored against his navel.

And what do I look like to you now, he said.

—

BETTER TO LOSE AN EYE

The envelope Lindsey pulled from the mailbox was an over-sized yellow square. It was addressed, in handwritten callig-raphy: *Lindsey Montgomery (and Parents)*. Standing in the driveway, the hot gravel biting her bare feet, Lindsey tore it open. The card inside was a giant sun with words printed over its smiling mouth. Lindsey hopped from foot to foot while she read.

Back-to-School Party!
Saturday, August 12, 5–8 P.M.
Madeline Seyler's house (call for directions)
Wear your swimsuit and bring a towel
RSVP 602-239-7646
Parents welcome to attend!

Lindsey tore the invitation and envelope into tiny squares, then buried the pieces beneath an egg carton in the outside trash can. She went inside and, using the polite language Nona taught her, left a message on the Seylers' voice mail. *Thank you for the kind invitation. We will be unable to attend.*

105

The next day Mrs. Seyler called. When Lindsey answered, she asked to speak to Lindsey's grandmother. Lindsey brought the phone to Nona.

Nona listened. She said, "No, I hadn't heard." She said, "Thank you, we will," and put the phone down.

She looked at Lindsey. "Why didn't you tell me about the pool party?"

"I told Mama," Lindsey lied, looking at her mother, who was asleep in her wheelchair in front of the TV. She was wearing an orange skullcap pulled low over her ears. Lindsey could hear the heavy, low rasp of her breathing.

"Well, we're going," Nona said. "All three of us."

They drove to the party in the new van. Nona liked driving it. She said the van was a smooth ride and it was a blessing never to have to worry about parking. Next to Nona, Lindsey's mother sat in her wheelchair, which locked into place with clamps built into the van's floor. She was wearing her red cowboy hat.

In the backseat, Lindsey sat with legs crossed underneath her terry-cloth cover-up. Her stomach felt like it might take off. None of the other kids had seen Mama the way she was now: the swath of scar and hollow dent at the base of her neck, the round bag of urine, the inward sag of her feet in their hot-pink Converse high-tops. Lindsey knew that before the party was over she'd have to say the words *tracheotomy* and *quadriplegic*. She'd have to say things like "Nona dresses her," "It goes into her bladder bag," "shot in the throat." And she'd have to say the thing she hated more than anything else to say: "She'll always be that way."

Madeline's house was white stucco with orange tiles on the roof and giant palm trees in pots on either side of the front door. Nona parked the van in the driveway and Lindsey stepped out onto the asphalt.

"Go on in and find Mrs. Seyler," Nona said, handing her a tray with carrot and celery sticks arranged in a circle. "Make sure she knows we brought this." Good—now she wouldn't have to walk into the backyard alongside Mama. Lindsey turned toward the side gate, onto which someone had taped a sign: *Arcadia Christian School 4th graders—Come On In!* She balanced the tray so the ranch dip in the center didn't spill over.

But Mama, her chair lowering from the van onto the driveway, said, "Give the tray to me."

Lindsey was startled by the choke in her own throat. These little bullet-bursts of rage toward her mother always startled her and she hated herself for them. Mama couldn't help what had happened to her. At night, when Nona lifted Mama onto the hospital bed they'd set up in the laundry room downstairs and Lindsey lay curled at her feet, listening to the scrape of her breathing—then she felt sorry for her, so sorry she would cry, crawl up the mattress and stroke her mother's long blond hair. One night Mama said she wished someone would paint clouds on the ceiling, and Lindsey promised she would do it when she turned ten, because then she'd be old enough, Nona would let her stand up on the tall ladder. At night, with Mama lying asleep in bed like anyone else's mother, Lindsey knew she would do more than paint ceilings for her, more than stroke her hair. If she could—if someone covered her own face with a pillow and held a gun to her head the way

Marcus had done to Mama—Lindsey felt she would die for her mother.

But now, hearing the whir of the wheelchair coming up the driveway, she felt the heavy drag in her stomach, the disgust. Not for her mother, really, but for parts of her, the things that were changed: the pasty skin, the crazy hats she wore, the latest tattoo, a flaming sword that reached from her right shoulder blade ("I can't feel the needle," she'd said, "so I might as well") to the snarled curve of her upturned fingers. Lindsey had seen a dead crab once on the beach in San Diego, its belly bared and bleached pinkish-white in the wet sand. While she watched, a wave came in and pushed it and made the claws move, only a little, but enough to suggest life, enough to make Lindsey walk over and toe the belly with the tip of her sandal. But it was long dead and the shell had cracked into fragments and there was nothing inside, only sand and seaweed and a few threads of what looked like stringy gray snot. It was sickening. The pieces lay there in the sand, the claws scattered, it was only the waves that moved them and that's how it was, now, with her mother's hands, whenever Lindsey moved them for her, helped her raise the spoon attachment to her mouth or wrap her fingers around the stick control of her chair. When Mama reached the top of the driveway Lindsey took her mother's hand off the stick and placed it in her lap, watching it bend back into its familiar ruined shape. She set the tray on top of the hands, loathing them.

Nona came up the driveway with the pool tote in which Lindsey had packed her towel and goggles. "Here," she said, handing her the bag. "I'll push." Lindsey opened the gate and held it while Nona guided her mother inside, then she followed them down a flagstone path. Lindsey jogged a bit to keep up. Nona was a retired hippie. She'd had Mama when she was only eighteen, with a mistake-of-a-boy. And then, she said, came her three Rs: she repented, got reborn, and retired her old ways. But she kept the look; she wore long skirts and didn't cut her hair until a month after Mama's accident, when she came home with it sculpted into little arrows pointing in toward her face. Nona showed Lindsey her long brown braid, rubber-banded and sealed in a Ziploc, which she slid into a padded envelope addressed to *Locks of Love*. In her bedroom that night, Lindsey cried when she thought about the braid, curled up in the baggie like a severed tail. She cried for the little girls with cancer who would have to wear wigs made of Nona's hair, cried because what Nona had done was beautiful, because of how tall and startled Nona looked in short hair.

"Look at this place," Nona said now, in the chipper way she talked to Mama. "Can you believe it? Think where you were a year ago, shut up in that laundry room, no way to get anywhere. And now that blessed van . . . God is faithful. He is Jehovah-Jireh." She stopped pushing for a minute to raise her hands, palms toward the sky.

Nona was convinced the van was an answer to her prayer for Mama's trapped essence to come out. "I've had this vision," Nona told Lindsey the day they brought Mama home from the Care Center. "Your Mama's trapped in an ugly bottle. And the spirit inside is beautiful, full of swirling rainbow colors. We've just got to get the cork out."

But for the next year Lindsey's mother couldn't go anywhere unless Nona called Dial-A-Ride, which came late or didn't come at all. And Mama refused to talk to anybody but Lindsey and Nona—not even the nurses who circled in and out of the house in their white coats and soft shoes like figures on a carousel. "I hate my voice now," she told Lindsey. She wouldn't listen to the taped police interview during Marcus's trial and she made Nona throw out all her karaoke CDs. Lindsey had loved when her mother sang karaoke, the mic in one hand and a beer in the other. Her hair hung to her waist and had pink and blue streaks running through it. Sometimes she stopped singing mid-song, with the words still scrolling up through the screen; she closed her eyes and moved her hips to the music. She taught Lindsey to swear and let her do it in the car, in the apartment, anytime she wanted, as long as Nona wasn't around.

But Nona said, "You're ruining that child." She said it right in front of Lindsey. "Dyeing her hair, leaving her alone with Marcus. There comes a time"—she was on her knees, cleaning the tub in the small bathroom Lindsey shared with her mother in their old apartment—"when the generational cycle has got to be broken."

Lindsey had liked Marcus—he played Xbox with her and drew fake tattoos on her kneecaps. But Nona had been right about him. And she was convinced she was right about the van's being the answer to her prayer for the uncorking. It would begin today, she'd said at breakfast, pointing her fork toward some invisible evidence behind and to the right of Lindsey's head. At the pool party. The other parents, the *compassionate* parents who'd helped raise the money for the van and for Lindsey's tuition, would ask questions; they would all want to talk to her, hear her story. She would be forced out of her shell. "No one can ignore that toxic green wheelchair," Nona had said.

But that wasn't really the color, Lindsey thought now, looking at Mama's chair resting half on and half off a rectangular slab of flagstone. It was more of a mint green.

"The mountain's so close," Mama said, her body listing sideways. "I want to see." Nona took off Mama's hat so she could get a better look at Camelback. Lindsey looked too; the red rock mountain she'd seen only from a distance when they took the freeway to school now loomed, rugged and bare. It was all scrub brush and creosote, not the pale fur Lindsey had once imagined would cover the peak in soft tufts.

"There's the Praying Monk," Lindsey said, pointing to the rock formation that looked like a hooded figure kneeling to face the camel. Mama once told her the legend—how the monk was the first Spanish missionary to arrive in Phoenix. How he and his camel (and here she explained that, of course, there hadn't *been* camels in Arizona, it was just a story they made up because of the shape of the mountain) traveled for days through the desert until they ran out of water. Still they walked, until the camel fell to its knees. And the monk, dying of thirst himself, did the only thing he could—he bowed down in front of his camel and prayed for a miracle. And God heard, but even He couldn't make water spring from desert rocks. Instead, out of mercy, He turned them both into stone, to save them and put an end to their suffering.

The Seylers' backyard was bigger than any yard Lindsey had seen. They followed the path past a tennis court and a two-story Victorian playhouse and into a grassy courtyard with a fountain made of sculptured fish. And then Lindsey could see, from the way Nona stopped abruptly in front of the fountain, that something was wrong.

The swimming pool was not on ground level. It was up a flight of marble stairs—six steps, a landing, then six more. The kids and parents were all up there. Mr. Seyler was grilling; kids were lining up at the diving board.

"Lindsey." Nona's voice was sharp. "Take the vegetables up there." Lindsey took the tray from her mother's lap, trying not to look at her face or at the hands, but focusing on her mother's tank top. I'M IN IT FOR THE PARKING, the shirt said. Mama was braless; her breasts lay in flattened heaps beneath the ribbed fabric. Lindsey turned and ran up the stairs.

"Linds!" Madeline's blue goggles peered over the edge of the pool. "Come swim with us!"

Lindsey thought she might raise her own palms in gratitude. She would go back and kiss each marble step. Mama would have to stay down in the courtyard, corked in her bottle.

Inside the pool house, a ceiling fan blew air-conditioned currents around the room. Lindsey tried not to think about her mother, down there in the sun. Her skin would blister if she was out for too long; her body couldn't regulate temperature anymore.

"Hi, honey," said a lady with glasses and freckled skin. "Just set those anywhere. You must be Valerie's daughter?" Lindsey nodded. "I'm Mrs. Seyler. Was your mother able to make it?"

"She's down with my grandma."

"Oh my *God*," said Mrs. Seyler, slapping a hand to her forehead. "The steps—I forgot."

Lindsey set the vegetable tray on a table and went outside. The pool was dark blue with pearly-pink swordfish tiled into the steps. Fountains ran down into the deep end from the Jacuzzi; kids were jumping off the ledge in between. Lindsey took off her cover-up and dipped a foot in. She should just jump. But she noticed Mrs. Seyler talking to Mr. Seyler, who set down his spatula and took off his big silver glove. And now they were going down the stairs, down to where Mama and Nona were hunched in the thin shade of a mesquite tree.

"Lindsey, come on!" Madeline's face floated beneath her. "Jump!"

Lindsey hesitated, then plugged her nose and stepped off the edge. She sank fast and hard; it was easy to sit on the bottom. She stayed there for as long as she could, watching tiny bubbles float to the surface. It was warm underwater—too warm—and the chlorine stung her eyes. But it was quiet and she was hidden. She sat until her chest burned for air. *This is what it feels like to suffocate. This is what it's like.*

She pushed off and shot to the surface.

Madeline, Keri Johnson, and a boy she didn't recognize were hanging on to the edge of the pool. "Geez," said the boy. "How'd you hold your breath that long?"

Lindsey grabbed onto the side next to Madeline.

"Hey, Lindsey," Keri said, swimming around to Lindsey's other side. "It's cool we're in class together again. Mrs. Collins gives out Funny Bucks if you do extra-credit stuff."

"What's Funny Bucks?" Lindsey asked. Last year Keri had whispered things about Lindsey's mama to some of the other girls: *She does drugs. Had a fight with her boyfriend.*

"It's fake money," Keri said. "You get to buy candy at the end of the year."

The boy grabbed a yellow foam noodle off the deck and tucked it under his arms. He floated around in front of Lindsey and raised his goggles. "You're that girl with the mom who got shot in the neck." He swam closer. His eyes were huge, surrounded by dented red circles. "Did an ambulance come and get her?"

"Helicopter."

"Cooool. Did it just, like, land in your backyard?"

"It was an apartment."

"Leave her alone, Brendan," Madeline said.

Brendan started to push the surface with his palm, making ripples and waves, never taking his eyes off Lindsey. "Did you see her, after? I mean, when she was, you know. All bloody?" Madeline and Keri hung from the side, goggles fixed on Lindsey's face.

"I was asleep."

"But didn't you, like, hear it?"

Lindsey didn't answer.

"So can her wheelchair stand up?" Brendan asked. "I saw this guy at the store once, he just pushed a button and he could get stuff off the top shelf."

"She can't get stuff off a shelf," Lindsey said. "She's a *quadriplegic.*"

"Want to go off the diving board?" Madeline said.

"Yeah, let's go." Keri was now on her side. They swam to the ladder in the deep end and climbed out. Keri had on the two-piece swimsuit Lindsey had wanted at Old Navy, with a palm tree and setting sun and the word *Malibu* on the butt. Nona made her buy a one-piece. It was plain blue and the only cute thing about it was a row of rainbow-colored beads strung onto the left shoulder tie.

"Hey, Keri—what's your dad doing down there?" Madeline was leaning over the marble rail, pointing down into the courtyard. Keri's father was standing with Mr. Seyler next to Mama's wheelchair. Other dads were down there too—they were talking with Mr. Seyler and gesturing. Lindsey saw her mother's cowboy hat bob.

"My mom can't get up the stairs," Lindsey said.

"Do you still want to dive with us?"

"I'm just going to get a tube," Lindsey said. She headed toward a blow-up ring near the shallow end; when the girls weren't looking, she grabbed her towel and ran down the steps.

". . . God's mighty arms," she heard Nona say when she reached the mesquite tree. "His people do for the weak what they can't do for themselves." Lindsey came up and took Nona's hand, and Nona leaned down and whispered, "Didn't I tell you? It starts today!" From where she stood Lindsey couldn't see her mother's face; her head was bowed beneath her hat.

"I think four of us," Mr. Seyler said, "two to a side, should do it. Let's give it a try."

They lifted. Nona hid her eyes, but Lindsey watched, motionless. She knew the wheelchair was heavy—three hundred pounds, with Mama in it. But they got it up off the grass, a good two feet. She could see the muscles ripple in Mr. Seyler's back, faces turning red, veins popping. When they set her back down Mama's body shimmied with the impact.

"All right, let's push her to the staircase."

"Let me go on ahead," Nona said. "I can't bear to watch." She put a hand on Mama's shoulder. "Jesus, lift this child up. Little ones to Him belong, they are weak but He is strong." Lindsey watched her hurry away across the grass, light as air, lovely, her Keds flashing white beneath her long skirt.

Lindsey stayed next to the chair as the men pushed it toward the stairs. "Mama?" she whispered. "Are you sure this is safe? What if they drop you?"

"Yeah, might break my neck, wind up paralyzed," Mama whispered back. She paused to breathe. "Go up with Nona."

Lindsey stayed where she was. Who else would catch Mama if she fell? She watched the men lift, watched the chair tilt with every step, the round bag of urine in its black zippered case swinging like a pendulum. The dads set Mama down on the landing and rolled their shoulders. On the second flight, a front wheel bumped one of the steps. The jolt knocked Mama's cowboy hat off, leaving the roots of her hair exposed, dark and flecked with dandruff.

When they reached the top, a few people applauded. The men smiled at one another, shaking out their arms. Madeline's dad patted Mama's lower arm while Lindsey trudged up the steps, stopping to pick up the hat. "Let's get you into the shade, hon," Nona said. "Let's get your water bottle refilled. We can't have a dry throat today." Nona put Mama's hand on the control stick so she could drive, then led the way.

"Wait," Lindsey said, following them. "She needs her hat."

Everybody started filing through the pool house, loading plates with food: hot dogs, hamburgers; salads topped with candied walnuts, dried currants, strawberries, and feta cheese. A row of "Fat-Free!" and "Light!" and "No Oil!" salad dressings, pot stickers, fruit trays, risotto, deviled eggs sprinkled with parsley, organic blue corn chips, homemade guacamole. Nona's carrot-and-celery tray with its plastic tub of Hidden Valley ranch dip sat untouched.

When Lindsey came out of the pool house, she saw that Nona had parked Mama under a covered portico at the far end of the pool and surrounded her with a circle of chairs. The chairs were empty.

Lindsey felt her cheeks grow hot. It was one thing to ignore Mama when she was down in the courtyard; it was another thing to ignore her now. She found Nona sitting with a group of women in jeweled flip-flops and Capri pants. "The first time I truly identified with Mary the mother of Christ," Nona was saying, "was looking at those crumpled hands. It was like I wanted to throw my mantle over my face and go hide in a cave. Now where did that vision come from?" The women listened politely, placing small forkfuls of salad in their mouths. Among these women Nona looked even younger. She could have been one of them, mother of a fourth-grader.

Lindsey tugged on Nona's sleeve. "No one is sitting with Mama."

Nona wrapped her arm around Lindsey's waist and pulled her close. She went on talking, plate balanced on her lap. "I asked the doctor that day," she said, "'Doctor, is she going to be this way for the rest of her life?' and the doctor said"—Nona paused, looking around the circle—"he said, 'Yes. And for the rest of yours.'"

"Bless your heart," said Mrs. Seyler. "I can't imagine what it must be like for you."

"Nona," Lindsey said. "Mama is alone."

Nona gave her a squeeze. "Why don't you go sit with her," she said. "I'll be over in a minute." She picked up her fork and Lindsey saw Nona's hand was shaking. When she tried to take a bite of her salad, she knocked the plate off her lap.

Nona hardly ever left the house. Now she was the one coming uncorked.

"Let me get that," one of the mothers said.

"It's fine," Nona said, bending over to pick up the plate; when she sat up her eyes were wet.

Mrs. Seyler looked at Lindsey. "That's a cute swimsuit," she said. "I like the beads."

"I'll tell you what, though," Nona said. "I'll take Valerie this way over the way she was before. The drugs and alcohol, boys, constant parties. Thank God Lindsey was asleep when Marcus—"

"Nona," Lindsey said. She stepped away from the circle. "Let's go sit with Mama now."

Nona stood up. "There's that verse," she said, setting her plate on the chair, "and it's the truth: 'Better to lose an eye than to have the whole body thrown into Hell.'"

Lindsey couldn't stand it any longer. "That's *bullshit*!" She heard her own voice explode above her head somewhere. "It's not her eye, it's her *whole fucking body*!"

Nona covered her mouth with her hand.

The mothers looked down at their plates; some of them looked away. Mrs. Seyler stood and tried to put an arm around Lindsey, but she ran before anyone could touch her. She ran past the pool, past Madeline and Keri. She ran past Brendan and some other boys who sat on their towels eating. She ran to the portico, to the empty chairs, to Mama. She loved her, loved her desperately; she would sit with her, facing her, her back to the party, to the world. She would hold Mama's crumpled hands, she would kiss them, she didn't care who saw. They would sit there together, the two of them, with only the blue sky and clouds drifting overhead. They would sit there until God had mercy and turned them both to stone.

GEORGIA THE WHOLE TIME

Dying, I tell Neil, is like driving south up a mountain.

"58 South," I say as we start the ascent on the way home from the clinic in Chattanooga. "We're going *south* and driving *up*."

"Sandwich walks into a bar," Neil says. His hands open and close around the steering wheel.

But the metaphor is too good to let go. "Like me. Uphill climb, body heading south all the while."

"And the bartender says, 'I'm sorry, we don't serve food here.'"

Thirty seconds later Neil says, "And by the way. You're not going to die." His timing is off—it sounds like the punch line.

We moved from Phoenix to Lookout Mountain, Georgia, eight months ago, so Neil could teach economics at Westminster College. You can see the tower on the north end of Carter Hall from anywhere on the mountain. Most people think the tower is some kind of theological statement: aspiration toward God, beacon-on-the-hill. But back during Prohibition, Carter Hall was a luxury hotel and speakeasy. The tower was built to keep a lookout for the authorities.

Unless there's a truck in front of you, it takes seven minutes to drive up from Chattanooga to the top of Lookout. When you cross the Tennessee/Georgia line, the trees open up so you can see the view beyond the rusted guardrail. WELCOME—WE'RE GLAD GEORGIA'S ON YOUR MIND, the sign says. But Georgia isn't on my mind. What's on my mind is the cliff on my left and the sheer limestone wall on my right.

At the top is the town of Lookout Mountain, Georgia. Turn right, drive four blocks, and you're in Lookout Mountain, Tennessee. Two states, one town. Population, just over five thousand. The two-state thing was a selling point with the kids. "You can trick-or-treat in Georgia *and* Tennessee," we told them.

Some houses span the border. In these cases, state of residence depends on the master bedroom: if it's in Georgia, then you live in Georgia, even if the rest of the house is in Tennessee. The story goes that one man spent a year converting his garage into a master suite because he wanted to live in Tennessee, where there's no state income tax. After he'd changed his address and moved his furniture, he found his property taxes had doubled.

It doesn't matter which side you choose, our realtor said. It all evens out.

Our realtor also said the master bedroom rule isn't accurate in the *scientific* sense, since statistics show that, assuming an average life span, when you die you will have spent only a third of your time asleep. State of residence, he said, should depend on the room with the television.

A third of the time asleep. So what I'm losing is only two-thirds.

*   *   *

We decided to move to Georgia last March, before I found out that my melanoma had recurred. By June—when I found out—the house in Phoenix had sold and the car was packed. The contractor had installed French doors in the new house; Myra had picked petal pink for her walls.

I had surgery the day after the diagnosis. What I was hoping to hear, what I'd heard the first time, was *in situ*. This time, Dr. Planer didn't say *in situ*. She said *stage four*. It was Neil's last day at work, and the day before the first leg of our drive, and the last day on our current insurance. How could I help thinking the timing was perfect?

While the surgeon scooped out tissue in my lower arm, he talked about increased family risk. "You need to contact your siblings. Do you have siblings?" Right, siblings. There are four of us. Of whom I am the eldest. The one who is supposed to take care of the elderly parents—when they become elderly. My parents are in their late fifties.

"And we're not just talking sunscreen with the kids," the surgeon said. "We're talking indoors."

I said, "We're moving to a mountain near Chattanooga. It's shady there."

"You're lucky," the nurse said. "I'd give anything to get my boys out of this sun."

I closed my eyes against the smoke from the cauterizer. "I know," I said. "The whole thing is really providential."

Acknowledging you are dying is the first step toward living the rest of your life.

I have not acknowledged anything to anyone but Neil. Moving was hard enough. I wear long sleeves, and I've been lucky with the hair. Hyperthermic isolated limb perfusion—where

121

they cut off the circulation in my arm with a tourniquet and inject the warmed chemo—does not involve hair loss.

But at the clinic today, they implied it might be time to start acknowledging. There are, they said, satellite tumors.

And they gave us—Neil and me—the helpful booklet. *Even before you show signs of serious illness, people may have a different look in their eyes when they talk to you.* And, *Don't be afraid to ask to be alone.*

We pick up the kids from school on our way home. Grady throws his backpack into the car before he climbs in. "TGI*Thur*," he says. Tuesdays he says TGI*T*. This is what happens when you teach a four-year-old his days of the week and his consonants at the same time.

Myra keeps her backpack on. "How come you're driving us?"

"Hey, you two," Neil says. "I forget. What's the guy's name with no arms and no legs, hanging on the wall?"

"Art!" Grady yells.

"No arms, no legs, swimming in a lake?"

"Bob!" he yells again.

"Don't you have classes?" Myra asks.

"Canceled," Neil says. "On account of ice cream."

Our realtor did not tell us about the leash laws. The Tennessee side has a leash law; the first walk I took on the Georgia side, three dogs followed me home. The Georgia dogs have stamina.

Every time I hear that another dog has been hit by a car, I know which side it lived on.

Last week, a big mixed breed scratched at my back door. His tag said *Bo, 5874 Cinderella Circle,* a cul-de-sac twelve blocks from our street. Twelve blocks used to be a warm-up. I looked for my car keys.

Bo's tail slapped the insides of my thighs when I rang the doorbell. A lady I recognized from church opened the door. I said, "Your dog came to my house and I thought I'd bring him home."

"Oh, he runs everywhere," she said. "But thanks for bringing him. Call next time—I'll come to you!"

Dogs are the kind of worry I can manage.

My kids worry about a tiny white terrier who crosses the street to meet us on the walk home from school. Yesterday, Myra screamed when a passing truck brushed the dog's tail. His fur is matted and he has a shrill, rapid-fire bark. He won't let me pick him up. The kids want to adopt him, but I tell them he already has a home. "Yah! Go home!" we shout, and stamp our feet at him, but this doesn't work. We decide our best bet is to ignore him. "Don't pet him, Grady," Myra says. "If you do, he'll follow us."

Yesterday, with the terrier barking at their shins, Myra took Grady's hand. "I bet you can't walk as fast as me. Come on, try to walk fast." She pulled him along and his mitten came off in her hand. Grady took off the other mitten and pitched it back across the street into the dog's front yard. "Get it, doggy!"

"Go pick up your mitten," Myra said. "Your fingers will freeze."

But I said to leave it. I said, "Grady, that was brilliant. Trying to save the doggy like that. You are a brilliant little boy."

When we get home, Neil runs the helpful booklet through the shredder and goes online. The NCI website keeps an updated list of clinical trials by state and region. There's a new study in Birmingham the oncologist thinks I'll qualify for. The drug is Interferon Alpha. Primary interference? Is this what I want to do, interfere primarily? It's something I'd say to a teenaged daughter: I have a right to interfere! I don't like the sound of it. Interfering is only rifling around in someone else's business. Interfering is not ending.

"We'd have to drive down three times a week," Neil says. "We could ask Sandra to walk the kids home from school." *Be grateful, and accept help, from whatever source, graciously.* But would Sandra let Grady pet the terrier? Would she make him go back for his mitten?

In bed, Neil wants to stroke my skin. He tells me it's soft as butter. Like feathers. Like fluffy clouds.

And I say things I never used to say. Why don't I dance naked for you. Why don't I lick you, suck you, sit on you. Why don't we do it on the dresser. In the rocking chair. Why don't you have your way with me.

You won't hurt me, I say.

Our next-door neighbor is a widow from Savannah. Her name is Anita, and she calls me *darlin'*. From my bedroom window, I always see her putting out leftovers on aluminum pie plates for the squirrels. Sometimes I go out back and we chat over the cedar fence that separates our side yards while she walks back and forth with her metal detector. She puts the things she finds in a cake pan on her deck, then sells them to the Point Park Museum. Since I've known her, she's found half a rusted canteen and three broken Confederate belt buckles.

Point Park is on the Tennessee side, where the east and west brows of the mountain come together. Billboards along 58 South have photographs of actors dressed in Civil War uniform: COME VISIT POINT PARK, WHERE THE BATTLE BEGINS EVERY 30 MINUTES! This is false advertising. You think you're going to watch a live reenactment, but it turns out to be an electronic battle map presentation.

We took Myra and Grady to see the battle map our second week here. We sat in theater chairs in front of a room-sized model of Chattanooga, with lines of toy blue and gray soldiers in formations around the city. I thought the soldiers would move, but once the presentation started a series of tiny lights underneath them—red for Confederate, blue for Union—blinked on and off in synch with the narration. We watched the rows of lights ascend and descend Lookout Mountain and Missionary Ridge. Grady fell asleep until the Rebel yell woke him up and made him cry.

After the presentation, you have to exit through the gift shop, which is divided the same way the mountain is: Tennessee souvenirs, Georgia souvenirs. We bought strictly Tennessee, since that was the state we were *visiting*. Grady picked a bag of cast-iron soldiers; Myra chose a mug that said *American by birth, Southern by the grace of God*. Neil bought a tall shot glass with three fill-lines. Fill it to the top, you're a Rebel; fill to the middle, you're a Southern Belle; fill only to the bottom line, you're a Yellow-Bellied Yank.

The Georgia side of the gift shop was all garden gnomes, birdhouses, snow globes with forest animals posed in front of cottages, handmade quilts, and fudge. Walker County has chosen to highlight the natural beauty of the mountain. The only tourist attraction on the Georgia side is a fairy tale–themed park called Rock City Gardens. Our subdivision is called Fairyland Farms; Myra and Grady go to Fairyland School. They pronounce it "*feh*-re-lind." Even the streets have fairy tale names:

125

Robin Hood Trail, Tinkerbell Lane, Mother Goose Avenue. My favorite is a nod to Shakespeare—Puck Circle. You can imagine the graffiti.

On the Tennessee side, the streets are named after Confederate generals.

Friday morning, Grady wants to take his plastic infield rifle for show-and-tell. I am certain I read *No toy weapons* in the pre-K handbook.

"Ned brought in a broken gun from the war," Myra says. "His dad dug it up in his backyard."

"I don't think you'll have show-and-tell," I say. "Today's the Valentine's party."

On the way to school, Grady picks up a cone-shaped magnolia seedpod and shoves it into his backpack. "Grenade," he says.

In the '70s, back in Phoenix, our parents put zinc oxide on our noses so we wouldn't freckle. In the '80s, when people started worrying about ozone, we were teenagers. Our mothers said *skin cancer;* we turned up the radio.

When my parents call to ask how the treatment is going, I want to tell them it's not their fault: You tried to make me wear sunscreen and I refused. But the type of melanoma I've developed is genetic, with no proven link to sun exposure. So the truth is, it's my parents' fault after all.

What I do blame my parents for? Burying my cat before I came home from school so I never saw the body. Lying about the boy down the street who put a desk chair through his bedroom window and opened his wrists on the broken pane. Presenting me with a world devoid of suffering and calling the cover-up *love.* How am I supposed to talk about loss with

Myra and Grady, when my own childhood experience is only half the story?

My first boss out of college, a woman twice-divorced and living with a younger man, once told me *You lead a charmed life.* I thought: *But where can I go from here?*

Tonight Neil is taking me out to dinner for Valentine's Day. He always has students lined up to babysit; some of these girls are graduate students, only a few years younger than I am. Watching them lean their elbows on our kitchen counter to read the instructions I've written, or coming home to find them asleep on our couch, I analyze their hips, the skin on the backs of their arms, the angles of their shoulder blades. I am sizing them up for Neil. Which one could have children that would look the most like Myra and Grady?

My favorite, the one who's coming tonight, is a senior named Meg. She has a wide-open face, large breasts, and thighs that are too big for her calves and ankles. I am small-chested and have great legs. Meg is desirable in a way that won't remind Neil of me.

The doorbell rings and the kids fight over who gets to open the door. "*I'll* get it," I say.

Meg is standing on the front porch, holding up her left hand. "Ta da," she says.

"Congratulations," I say. "Neil didn't tell me you had a boyfriend." I examine the ring, a single emerald-cut diamond set in platinum. I notice a pale freckle just above the ring. I notice Meg's French manicure, her long nail beds, the dozen or so silver bangles on her wrist.

"Yeah, he's in school back home." She pulls a thick bride magazine out of her backpack. "Can Myra stay up to help me look at dresses?"

"How come Myra gets to stay up?" Grady says.

Myra says, "I get to wear my mom's dress when I get married."

My wedding dress is dated: the sleeves puff and the train gathers underneath an enormous blush-pink bow. Myra loves it now. But I know the only way she'd come to wear it would be as a tribute.

Neil takes me to Tony's. They serve garlic bread with whole cloves baked in, and pastas like pumpkin Gorgonzola ravioli.

"You need to eat," Neil says. "Force yourself."

But I'm thinking about Myra at the end of some flowered aisle, holding Neil's arm, wearing my wedding dress. "Make sure Myra knows she doesn't have to wear that dress," I say.

"You make sure," Neil says. "You're going to be there."

"She's been coming in to sleep with me during the night," I say. "This morning I woke up and found one of her hairs in my mouth."

Neil pulls his chair around to sit next to me. It's an awkward arrangement. The waiter stumbles on Neil's chair leg when he brings us the dessert menus. Neil pulls me to him, cups his hand around my upper arm, a single parenthesis. "Tell me what to do," he says. "How to act." Against my back, his arm is shaking.

"I don't know. Take it seriously. Help me tell the kids."

He puts his lips to my ear. "What's thin, brown, and sticky?" he whispers. The sensuality of his lips and breath is startling, incongruous. I don't answer. "A stick," he says. He takes off his glasses. Then, sliding his wine out of the way, he leans over and rests his forehead on the tablecloth. He reaches for my hand. I can tell he's crying by the way his shoulder blades keep contracting beneath his shirt.

I lean into him, press my breasts into his back. Before, I would not have believed that it's possible to feel arousal and despair at the same time. That you could want to straddle your husband across a restaurant chair, open your blouse, rock in his lap and cry with pleasure, cry because now you know, you *know* how much you love your body and his. Only they're less and less yours every day. You cry because this last raw thing—fucking—has become a consolation. You cry because when your husband first makes love to another woman, it will be a consolation. And then, later, it won't.

On Sunday morning I wake up early—there's a chocolate Lab barking at a squirrel in the crab apple. I go out front and check its tag. *Missy, 406 Peter Pan Rd.*

Anita, still in her nightgown, is sitting on her front porch. She waves and pats the chair next to her. "Wouldn't you like to come sit?"

It's warm out for February; Anita's barefoot. We talk about the Georgia dogs. Her husband used to be mayor on the Tennessee side, and were he still alive he'd push for a leash law in Georgia. "The way they get things done in Tennessee," she says. "Tennessee's a man's state, Georgia a woman's. Well, just look at the names."

I mention all the monuments in Tennessee, the obelisks engraved with *Ohio, New York,* and *Illinois.* I ask, "Why do they hold on to the whole Confederate thing? When it's all defeat?"

"Well now," she says. "But isn't that just like a man, to ignore his own surrender?" Her feet are smooth and white against the porch's brick floor.

"I'm dying," I say to her feet. "I have skin cancer and it's spreading. Neil wants me to do a clinical trial in Birmingham."

"Oh darlin'," Anita says. I feel her hand on my back. "Your husband told me you had cancer when you all moved in. I was wondering if you might not mention it sometime."

Beneath the crab apple tree, Missy has not stopped barking. She circles the trunk until the squirrel leaps onto the limb of an oak and climbs out of sight.

When you're young, no one ever tells you that underneath everything you'll ever do—school, job, parenting—is appetite. That someday you will look at a seventy-two-year-old widow in her nightgown and think, *She is the winner; I am the loser.* And you would come out of your skin, you would crawl up into the sweaty warmth of her armpit just to be inside all that pulsing life.

What would you think of me if I told you that I'm jealous of my own daughter—the ropy muscles in her legs, her thickening hair, her becoming? What if you knew that if you and I met somewhere—in the produce aisle, at the ATM—I would imagine cutting your insides out and sticking them into my own body? Would you think differently about me if you knew I would do this in order to breathe the scent of Grady's skin for another morning?

When the pastor announces a death in our congregation, he uses Saint Paul's metaphor: "Tom Huskins finished his race last Wednesday." As a runner, I have always liked the image. That would be the thing to think, on your deathbed—that at the end of yourself, you still had control. But now I see the metaphor only works for people who live to old age. They get to run the whole course.

I have started writing out my prayers, word for word, in a journal. Yesterday I copied down a psalm because it was easier than coming up with my own words. "Unite my heart, that I may fear your name" is what the psalm said. But when I opened my journal this morning, I saw that I'd written "Un*tie*." So what does that mean? Am I coming together, or splitting apart?

Sunday evening we tell the kids.

From small children, the question "Where do dead people go?" may not be a question about the afterlife, but about the physical body. First, try to answer with "They go into the ground at the cemetery."

We take Myra and Grady to the downtown aquarium. A shipment of penguins arrived two weeks ago, and we stand in front of the new Plexiglas, shivering. The penguins jostle each other. Some shimmy through the water like silk. The children laugh at the way the penguins walk. They pull their arms inside their sweatshirts and waddle, shouldering one another into the rail.

When we come out, the sun over the Tennessee River is lowering behind a haze of shifting clouds. Filtered this way, it looks like the moon. "Bright for nighttime," Grady says. We don't correct him. We walk down to the riverfront and sit on a flat rock next to the water taxi. *Rides, $3.00.*

"Can we ride it?" Grady asks.

"Okay," Neil says. "But first Mommy and I want to talk with you guys about something."

"It says *No Fishing.*" Myra is pointing to a shirtless man fishing halfway down the bank. Three poles are wedged between rocks, lines cast out and dragged sideways in the current. The man casts and reels a fourth line. "Here, kitty kitty," we hear him say. He looks up. "Goin' to catch me a big cat," he calls up to us.

Neil pulls Grady into his lap. Myra sits cross-legged, facing us. "Remember last summer, when Mommy had to get stitches in her arm?"

"Lemme see the scar," Grady says.

I pull up my sleeve to show him, and he traces the pink line with his index finger. I cannot feel his touch.

"That was cancer," Myra says. "They took it out."

"Well, last Thursday the doctors found some more. And this time they might not be able to take it out." Myra's eyes go wide.

"There's a doctor in Alabama who wants to try some new medicine," I say. "Daddy and I are going to drive down three days a week. We thought we'd have Sandra walk you home from school."

I'd assumed it would be Myra who asked the question, but it's Grady: "Are you going to die?"

I think of everything I could say. I knew a lady once who beat it. Breast cancer, stage four, lived fifteen years longer. I think of the story of Hezekiah, God prolonging his life, making the sun retreat up the steps.

Neil tells the truth. "Anyone here who *isn't* going to die, raise your hand!" Both their hands shoot up. Then Myra pulls hers down. "That's not the right answer," she says, and starts to cry. I take her onto my lap. We hold them and watch the man bring in a fish. He twists out the hook with a pair of pliers, then tosses the fish into a bucket.

Tell me if you think this is true: it is easier to accept defeat and try to make the wreckage look beautiful than to keep fighting and lose. It feels true to me.

"Battling" cancer is only a small, daily choice you make to live with dissonance, the melody of your life running one way, the bass of your thoughts running another. Someone says *tomorrow*, you hear *if*. Forgetting is a blessing you have to manufacture.

When I blow them kisses at bedtime, Myra and Grady snatch them out of the air and tuck them under their pillows to save till morning. And on our drives home from Birmingham, I make Neil take the back way up the mountain. Nickajack Road starts in Flintstone, Georgia, and winds up behind the college. It takes twice as long as 58 South. But there are no signs about battles. You're in Georgia the whole time.

SINKHOLE

When the camp director introduces God, he reminds us the man is just an actor.

"His real name is Frank Collins," the director says. "He lives in Knoxville and has a wife and three grown-up children." He looks down at the little kids on the benches up front. "I want to make sure you know this, so you don't get scared."

God comes out from behind a screen set up at the front of the open-air gym. He's wearing a dark navy sheriff's costume. He's short and muscular with a thick gray beard and buzz cut. He asks the kids in the front row to move—they scramble to the wood floor—then drags the bench forward and stands on it. He pulls a sheriff's hat from behind his back, molds the brim, and sets the hat on his head. From where I'm sitting, fourth row, I can see the tips of his white sneakers sticking out from beneath his pant legs.

"The name's God," the sheriff says. "You all don't need to tell me your names 'cause I got 'em written down in my book."

He hooks his thumbs over his belt. "Will you look at me up here on my cosmic cloud? A-peerin' down with my eagle eye at all of *you*."

On *you*, he quick-draws a pistol from inside his waistband. It's a cap gun, silver paint flaking off the barrel. He makes a show of opening and inspecting the cylinder, then snaps it into place and squints, his jaw moving like it's working tobacco.

"You there, sister," he says, aiming at a girl in my row. "How'd you like to have the flu, honey?"

He fires. Bodies jump.

"And I got cavities for *all* you all," he says. "This'll teach you not to mess around doing your homework on the Sabbath." He waves his gun over us like a wand, opening fire.

In my head I repeat the line my therapist gave me: I am my own Great Physician.

The tingling in my chest starts up anyhow.

I look around to try to spot Wren. Sometimes even just seeing her helps. But I can't find her, so I move my hand up to the airspace in front of my pecs, in case I have to do the Gesture. It looks like I'm doing the air Pledge of Allegiance. This is my ready position.

This is not the Gesture.

Doing the Gesture = failure.

Doing the Gesture = letting the sinkhole be the boss of me.

Frank Collins twirls the gun around on his finger, then shoves it back into his waistband. "Remember," he says. "I got your names written in my big ol' book. And lemme tell you something: I wrote most of you off a long time ago."

He steps off the bench and backs away, frowning, until he's behind the screen.

136

The camp director says that Frank Collins—an actor, you remember—will be a bunch of different gods this week. Campers in grades 1–6 will vote on which god is the real one. The older campers will talk about the faulty theologies behind the fake gods. I'll be a sophomore this year, so the faulty theologies group will include me.

During the closing prayer, the tingling goes away. I keep my hand in the ready position, just in case.

I'm an amazing runner. The most amazing runner in our city, the absolute best the city of Chattanooga has ever produced. Benjamin Mills, one of our own, the newspapers say. We've never seen the likes of it. The length of his stride, the way he sucks oxygen, form and function melding in thrilling new ways. Whatever it is, it moves in him the way wind moves in trees.

And to think he's only fifteen!

I'm supposed to get even more amazing. I'm supposed to get so amazing that people will say, We have never seen this before in a human being, there has never been another distance runner like Mills, he's the best in the state of Tennessee and when he goes to college we'll say best in the nation, and someday, when we see him on television with the American flag wrapped around his body (look how amazing, he's not even sweating!) we'll say, We knew it, we've always known it: Benjamin Mills has given us a glimpse of the limitless perfections of God Himself.

The thing that will stop me from being amazing is this dime-sized spot of skin between my pecs. This spot of skin is like a scar that cannot be touched by anyone or anything. If anyone or anything puts even the slightest amount of pressure on this spot—if I even think about someone or something touching it—the sinkhole opens. The sinkhole is black and spirals down and open like a whirlpool: first through my skin, then through the tissues and pectoral muscles and on into the bones of my sternum, and if I don't lie down and do the Gesture to make it stop, it will get all the way to my heart and wrap around it and clamp down until my heart stops beating and I die.

What I do to make the sinkhole close is, I press my fingers together the way swimmers shape their hands into paddles. Then I lie down and massage the airspace an inch above the spot of skin. I move my hand in what you would call clockwise circles if you were standing above me, watching. It's like wiping down a counter. The faster I wipe, the faster the hole shrinks back into the dime-sized spot of skin.

The first time my parents caught me doing the Gesture I was twelve. I was bringing in the garbage pail and trying not to think about the spot on my chest. But trying not to think about something is the same as forcing yourself to think about it, and I ended up lying down right there in the driveway.

My parents took me to the emergency room, where the nurses hooked me up to heart monitors that showed everyone I wasn't having a heart attack. But because of my little brother Sam—born with a hole in his heart that four surgeries in eighteen months couldn't fix—they did all kinds of tests. They taped wires to my chest and attached them to a monitor I hooked onto my belt. I had to wear it around for a week. If I felt anything funny—*flubbing,* the doctor said, or *racing*—I was supposed to push a button on the monitor to start recording. When I got three recordings, I was supposed to unhook the monitor from the wires and dial an 800 number, then hold the phone up to the monitor and push *playback* so the monitor could send the sound of my flubbing and/or racing heart into a computer that would write down the patterns with one of those jittery robotic arms.

I never called the 800 number. I never felt any flubbing or racing.

I felt the sinkhole opening, but the doctor didn't say *spiraling* or *clamping down.*

For another test, I had to run on a treadmill set at a steep incline until my heart rate was 200 beats per minute. It took me a long time to get there. Dr. Logan, the cardiologist, kept calling me Lance Armstrong. "Faster, Lance," he'd say. "I'd like to get out of here before next week."

When my heart finally reached 200, I had to jump off the treadmill and lie on my back on a padded table. Dr. Logan said this is the most taxing thing you can do to a heart: take it from one hundred percent exertion to one hundred percent inertia. A nurse injected a dye into a vein in my arm. The dye made me taste metal and lit up all the pathways running in and out of my heart. An EMT was in the room, holding a defibrillator, just in case.

Dr. Logan said my pathways were clear as crystal. He said, "I've never seen a heart resume its resting rate that quickly."

My resting heart rate is 46 beats per minute.

In my prime it could drop into the 30s.

It's when I'm running that I feel God wants to tell me something. I feel he wants to tell me the Big Thing he has for me to do. It's like this secret mission that only someone who has been touched by the divine could possibly understand.

Writing down the words I hear during my runs is my assignment. Not God's assignment, the therapist's. My parents made me start seeing him every week when they found out about the Gesture. So far I've only written down one word: *You*. And I keep trying to tell my therapist that "heard" isn't right. I don't say "heard" because the sound isn't in my ears. It isn't a sound. It's this pulse or rhythm just below the prickling in my chest that I know has some meaning, and one of these days—if I can figure out the rest of God's words before the sinkhole takes over—I will know exactly what it is God wants me to do. The important thing is not to think about it. When I feel the words start to pulse in my chest, if I think about them, they disappear and I feel the sinkhole spiraling into my sternum, getting ready to wrap around my pumping heart. I have to figure out how to listen sideways, out of the corner of my eye.

My therapist says the worst thing I can do is fight the sinkhole, or pray that God will take it away. He says the way to be the boss of my sinkhole is to a) accept it; b) have compassion for it; and c) *let it happen*. He says if I do this, I'll find out the sinkhole doesn't have the power I think it does.

Sometimes my therapist has me play out my worst-case scenario: what do I think will happen if I don't do the Gesture?

"Easy," I tell him. "The sinkhole will squeeze my heart to death."

He says that is my surface fear.

"Okay," I say. "Then my deeper fear is dying, period."

After the sheriff-God, on the way back to our cabins, I see Wren at the snack table with some other freshman girls. She's wearing a tank top and jeans. Her bare arms start out in the darkness, white and smooth as the inside of a shell.

"Hey, Wren," I say.

"Benjy," she says. She says my name like she wants to keep it inside her mouth; I imagine the letters all curled up together on her palate. Wren's hair is the kind of silky blond that shouldn't be thick but is, so thick it's like a sheepskin rug you want to dig your toes into. When she goes back to her cabin I imagine she'll put on a white nightgown and kneel beside her cot to pray. Her prayers at Ethos are always humble and straightforward: Help us to see others as you see them. Give us your kind of love for people.

"So that sheriff's a no-brainer," Madeline Simpkins says. Madeline's one of these girls all the guys like—big chest, heavy eye makeup, obviously ready for whatever it is you want to do with her. "You'd think they'd want to, like, challenge us."

Wren is holding a little Styrofoam cup filled with popcorn. "I imagine Him that way sometimes," she says. "Like He's just . . . I don't know. Waiting to fire."

I don't say anything. Neither does Madeline. Wren and I have lived on the same street on Lookout Mountain since we were five, the year her parents found out she had a tumor in her uterus the size of a lemon. Some weird kind of cancer with a name like *mezzanine*. They had to take out all her reproductive parts plus her colon. After her surgeries her dad got her a new bike with training wheels. She'd ride around our neighborhood, bald-headed, a catheter bag dangling from her wrist. The next summer, she pulled me into the empty girls' bathroom at the Fairyland Country Club and lifted her shirt to show me the cloth-covered bag sticking out of a hole in her side. "This is how I go," she said. "I don't even have to sit down." Every summer after that, her parents were flying her somewhere to get a new surgery to try to fix her insides so she could at least have that bag taken off. None of the surgeries worked. I'm pretty sure they've given up. When we were in seventh grade, everyone started asking everyone else to go out. No one asked her. She told me that if Protestants had nuns, she'd sign up.

To look at her, you wouldn't know a thing had happened if it wasn't for the compression stocking on her leg. Something to do with the radiation killing all the lymph, or messing with the mechanism that makes the lymph move around. When she walks she has to kind of drag her leg along with her, one swollen foot pointing out to the side. That foot makes me want to lift her up and carry her anywhere she wants to go.

"A bunch of us are going down to the waterfront at midnight," Madeline says. "Swimsuits optional."

I look at Wren and raise my eyebrows up and down a few times, like, Hey baby *hey*.

"Right," she says, laughing. Which is exactly what I thought she'd say. Wren's the whole reason I came to camp. I'm in love with her. She doesn't know it and wouldn't believe me even if I told her, because of her missing parts and her swollen leg. But I'm so in love with her that I've decided to ask her to do a faith healing on me.

This is called being the boss of my sinkhole.

Because of the sinkhole I've never been with a girl. Never even hugged one close. Wren's the only girl I know who I think might be safe; who would treat me the same, even if she saw me doing the Gesture, because of what she's been through. Here's how I'm hoping things will go. I drop hints all week, tell Wren I'd like to talk to her about something. The last night of camp, I ask her to meet me somewhere private, maybe down at the waterfront late at night. She agrees. I tell her everything. She says she wants to help if she can. I take off my shirt and lie down. I say, Please don't touch my chest until I ask. She starts praying. I imagine she'll get her mouth down next to my chest, right above the dime-sized spot. Her breath will be warm and moist, a sweet citrus smell to it.

When I tell her I'm ready, she'll take a drop of the oil I brought in a tiny Advil container and place it, lightly, with just the tip of her pinkie finger, onto the spot. The most delicate laying-on-of-hands. She'll say, In the name of Jesus I command you. I might ask her to say some Latin I found on a Catholic website about exorcism—*In nominus Christos, Dominus vobiscum.* When she's finished I'll touch the spot with my own finger, to be certain it worked. And when I'm certain—when I can tell the sinkhole isn't going to open—I'll lay my entire hand on top of my chest and take a few deep breaths. Then I'll place Wren's hand over mine, to prove to myself I can handle the added weight, and to show Wren what she did for me.

The Presbyterians wouldn't tell us for sure if Sam went to Heaven when he died. I overheard the pastor telling my parents that it depended on whether or not Sam was one of God's chosen people.

"But I can tell you that the Scriptures are full of promises to children born into covenant families," he said. "And you are a covenant family, so in all likelihood Sam is with the Lord."

"Are we talking percentages here?" my father said.

"All I know," the pastor said, "is that if I get to Heaven and see every baby that ever died, I will say, God, you are so good. And if I get to Heaven and see only some of the dead babies there, I will say, God, you are so good. And if I get to Heaven and see not one dead baby there, I will say, God, you are so good."

We found another church. It's called Ethos. As in: the church needs a new ethos because the old one is screwed.

At breakfast, the camp director rings a brass bell hung up above the dining hall porch. Most of us line up long before he pulls the rope. We can see the food through the screens, already laid out on the tables: pancakes, sliced cantaloupe, scrambled eggs, grits. Above the tables are chandeliers made out of wagon wheels. Just inside the doors is a big speaker with a microphone. After the director rings the bell, he asks one of the high schoolers to step inside and say grace into the microphone so that everyone waiting on the porch can hear. The prayer is like this bribe: be quiet and listen and you'll get food.

This morning—our second morning at camp—the director asks Wren to say grace. The kids waiting in line move away as she walks toward the doors. Dragging her leg with her. When she gets close to me I see that she's wearing cutoff shorts and has her swollen foot stuffed into a flip-flop. Her toenails are painted pink.

She takes the mike and says one of her simple, direct prayers: Thank you for the hands that prepared the meal, use the food to strengthen our bodies, be present in our conversations around the table, amen. Maybe I should let her wing it when I ask her to pray for my sinkhole.

Inside, I sit at Wren's table, beside her. She's with Madeline and a couple of the guys on the McCallie cross-country team. They're talking about James, a freshman wrestler who's supposed to win state in the 103-pound class next year.

"Doesn't he normally weigh, like, 130?" Madeline is saying.

"He was going to be six feet," Ransom McGuire says. "Now he might not make it to five-eight. He's stunting his growth."

"Have you seen him eat?" Quentin Jenkins says.

"I hear he *doesn't* eat," Madeline says.

"I mean after a match," Quentin says. "He'll finish off two pizzas, then go home and put on this plastic suit and ride a bike in his living room. Dude's crazy."

Ransom looks at me.

"We're running the ridge at four," he says. "You coming?"

"I think I'll do my own thing," I say. Quentin and Ransom exchange a look and I can tell they've been talking.

I turn to Wren.

"You doing the ropes course this morning?" I ask.

"Not the cat pole," she says. "Maybe the V-swing or zipline. Are you?"

"No," I say. "I need to get a long run in." I take a deep breath. "But I was thinking, maybe we could take a walk later? Like, after lunch?"

"Sure," Wren says. "As long as we don't, you know. Hike." She tucks her feet under the bench and I feel her thigh press up against mine. She doesn't move it away. She probably doesn't even realize it's there, because of the stocking. My sinkhole tingles a little.

"Just a walk," I say. "Meet me at the waterfront at one."

"How far are you running today?" Madeline asks.

"Whatever I can do in two hours," I say.

"For Ben that's like twenty miles," Quentin says.

"A-ma-zing," Madeline says, blinking, her lashes black and clumpy. "The discipline you have."

"More like addiction," I say. What I don't say is that for approximately half the time I'm gone, I'll be lying on the ground, panting, making air circles above my chest.

* * *

After breakfast and the morning assembly, when the high schoolers head out to the ropes course, I go back to my cabin to change. It's only ten but already the heat is radiating up from the grass on the soccer field, the sun reflecting off the aluminum cabin rooftops. Inside the cabin are nine beds: eight twin cots plus a double for our counselor, Daryl, a philosophy major at Westminster who has an earring and a goatee and smokes pot inside his sleeping bag when he thinks we're all asleep.

I put on my running shorts and a singlet and lace up my shoes. Then I set my watch and start out at an easy 7:00 pace. By mile two I'll pick it up to 6:30; mile four, 6:00. These early minutes are the gray space, the bland miles I have to run through before the prickling starts and the God rhythms pulse in my heart and I have to trick myself into not listening.

My therapist says when this happens, it's the first hit of endorphins. It's not God, it's biology, he says.

My therapist is not a runner.

I head down the dirt access road, past the entrance sign with letters molded out of horseshoes. I reach the paved highway and run a mile and a half down a long incline, then turn left into the Little River Canyon National Preserve. We used to train out here in middle school. Two miles and I'll hit the footbridge that crosses to the trailhead.

I run beside the river. The water's shallow and mostly shaded, a few coins of sunlight on the surface. When I reach the bridge, I sidestep down the embankment and kneel beside the water for a drink. Then I dip my whole head in. Best way to keep from overheating is to keep your head cool.

I cross the bridge and start up the trail. I'm feeling strong. Invincible, even. I'm thinking, Best of the Preps newspaper article, scholarship to Stanford, Olympic trials. I picture other people watching me get these things: fans waving flags, my parents opening the *Times Free Press* to a full-sized picture of me on the front page of the sports section. My father saying, We knew it, we've always known it.

The trail hairpins back and forth. I'm going fast. My shoes kick up dust, leaves, small rocks. Any second now, I think.

I focus my thoughts on the spot of skin between my pecs. Nothing happens.

I push myself harder. The incline makes my calves burn. Along the side of my knee, all the way up to my low back, I can feel my IT band tightening.

Now, I think.

Now.

No prickling, no tingling.

I picture hugging Wren, her chest pressing against mine.

I imagine wearing a tie made out of lead.

Now.

I reach the top of the ridge and still nothing's happened. I stretch, then walk up to the cliff overlooking Trenton. I pull off my shirt and feel the sun fire up my back. My stopwatch reads 58:13. It should be happening.

I pull up a tall grass weed, feathery at the tip. Knowing what I'm about to do creates a little buzz in my skin. I rub the tip of the weed on my lips first, to test the pressure. Then I turn it over and, with the firm end of the stalk, poke the dime-sized spot.

And then I'm on the ground. The sinkhole is spiraling open. It's whirling fast, faster than usual, and it's like something is reaching up from beneath me, through my low back and spine and ribs, tugging down.

I get my hand in the ready position. I am my own Great Physician, I think. I am the boss. The sinkhole widens through my skin, numbing everything it touches. I start to move my hand in tiny circles. Not too much. I want to hear God first.

Here I am, I say. Tell me.

The sinkhole twists around in my pectoral muscles. I feel my throat start to close and I have to gasp a little for air.

Please, I say.

My heart sort of pauses, like it's thinking. Then I feel this giant flub: *You.*

You what, I say. My voice is dry and wheezy as an old man's.

You. You. You. The word repeats with each heartbeat. The sinkhole moves into my sternum and I hear a crackling noise, like breaking ice.

I move my hand faster.

You what.

The sinkhole is turning into a sphere, the size of an orange. I feel it fingering around, looking for my heart. *You you you.*

The corners of my vision are turning fuzzy gray. My chest burns. I've never let it get this far before.

You what—in my mind I fling the words up to God.

I feel the sinkhole grab my heart.

YOU you. Squeeze, release, like a handshake.

You what.

You you you

You—

My brother is lying in a clear plastic bassinet in a hospital room. I'm allowed to see him one last time and in my mind I know he's dead but while I look at him I feel this electricity jumping around inside my hands, like any second blue lightning is going to shoot out of my fingertips, which feel burnt.

And I think, If I touch him and say, Sit up, he will. I reach out my hand. Then I remember how God strikes people down for trying to mess with his decisions: Adam and Eve kicked out of Eden, Pharaoh and his army drowned in the Red Sea, Herod eaten up by worms. And when the nurse comes in to get me, I pull my hand away and walk out. I don't even say goodbye.

You could have.

When I wake up I'm on my back. My T-shirt is crumpled beneath my head. I don't know how long I've been asleep. I can tell that the sinkhole is still open, stuck inside my sternum, sitting there like an open wound. No pain or tingling, just this eerie numbness.

I stand up, dizzy. The sinkhole spirals around in my chest, slowly, like an old record.

I turn and sprint the downhill back to camp.

Wren, I think.

Wren Wren Wren.

When I get to the cabin, Ransom and Quentin are just leaving.

"Dude," Ransom says. "Daryl went to the staff lodge. I think he's calling your parents."

"You guys knew I went for a run," I say. The sinkhole is so wide I'm sure if I take off my shirt they'll see it gaping there, black and empty.

"Like, five hours ago," Ransom says. "We were heading out to look for you."

"I got turned around on the trails," I say.

"Your face is fried," Quentin says.

I grab my towel from the nail beside my bed, then kneel down and root around in my duffel as if I'm looking for my shower stuff. But I'm gathering my faith healing supplies: oil in its tiny Advil bottle, small New Testament bound in red leather, three votive candles, matchbook, flashlight. I wrap everything up in the towel, then go to the lodge to look for Daryl. I find him watching something on the staff television. He doesn't seem worried or mad when he sees me.

I tell him I got lost on the trails. I tell him I'm sorry and that I won't run alone again. I tell him I'll call my parents if he wants me to.

Daryl tilts his head back so he's looking at me down the bridge of his nose. "That girl came to find me," he says. "Wren. Said you guys were going to take a walk and you never showed."

"Like I say, I got lost," I tell him.

"She seemed genuinely worried," Daryl says.

"I'll talk to her tonight," I say. "I'm going to shower up and rest."

His eyes narrow. "Right on," he says. "Listen. I don't know what you've got going, but don't mess with that girl. She's good, you know?"

"I know," I say. He watches me walk out, so I turn toward the bathrooms. Then I circle around behind the lodge, take the rolled towel down to the waterfront, and stuff it deep in the bushes beside the canoe dock.

At the evening session in the gym, I find Wren sitting in the back row. She smiles and moves over a little when I walk up.

"What happened?" she says. "I waited till two."

"I'm sorry," I say, sitting beside her. "I got lost on this trail."

"Are you okay? You're all splotchy." She touches my cheekbone, just barely brushes it with the tip of her index finger.

The sinkhole spins around a few times. I suck a little air in between my teeth.

"There's something I need to ask you," I say.

Her eyes go wide. She looks down into her lap.

"I was thinking we could go down to the waterfront—" Before I can finish, Frank Collins comes out from behind the screen. He's wearing black pants and a white shirt with a bow tie. A kitchen towel is draped over his forearm; in his hands are a pencil and leather notepad.

"My sincere apologies for being late," he says, using a British accent. "I hadn't expected to come to work this evening."

Wren nudges me with her swollen leg. "A thousand bucks he's the Genie God," she says. Again she leaves her leg against mine, and the sinkhole deepens, *you, you* humming faintly.

When she looks away, I move my hand up to the ready position.

"Beg your pardon?" God says to no one in particular. "Ah, the menu. How silly of me to forget." He hands an imaginary menu to a little boy. "Now sir, the last time you were here, you ordered a win for your baseball team. Would you like another?"

The boy stares up at him.

"My apologies, sir, that item is not on the menu. But I'll see what I can do." He pauses, listening. "I know you can take your business elsewhere, and believe me when I tell you how much I appreciate your loyalty. It's just that I'm not entirely certain I can do what you're asking. No, please, sir, don't walk away. I rely on customers like you to stay in business. I might have to close up shop if I can't keep producing . . . I understand. No hard feelings. Know that I'm here, at your service, anytime you'd like to return."

The waiter hangs his head and sighs.

"My restaurant used to be so busy," he says. "Then again, there were far fewer restaurants to choose from. And people used to listen when I made recommendations." He walks back to the foldout screen, then turns to face us.

"I suppose I can't blame them for leaving," he says. "After all, I *am* just a waiter."

When he's gone and the camp director starts talking, I pull my hand down from the ready position and turn to Wren.

"Can you come to the waterfront with me?" I say. "I need your help with something."

Wren's chewing on her pinkie nail. "When?"

"Now," I say. "Right now."

"Can I meet you? I want to stop by my cabin first."

"Let's go now. I'll walk you to your cabin and wait." Wren's knees bounce; she keeps swallowing.

"And now," the camp director is saying, "before the music team comes up, we have another god."

"I'm going to stay and see this one," Wren says. "I'll meet you down there, okay?" As soon as she turns away my hand starts moving.

Frank Collins scuffs out in slippers. He's wearing Bermuda shorts hiked way up with a belt and has a pair of reading glasses down on the end of his nose. He keeps gumming his tongue, which rests on his lower lip. He sticks a pipe in his mouth, then takes it out, looking around like he's expecting something.

"Hold on," he says. "Lemme turn up my earpiece." He pretends to twist something in his ear. "My name?" He digs around in the pocket of his shorts. "This is why I keep my ID with me." He pulls out a card. "My name is . . . Blue Cross Blue Shield!"

Laughter.

"That ain't right," he says, feeling in his pocket again. "Ah, here it is. My name is American Express!"

More laughter. God smacks his lips. "Well, never mind who I am. It's more important what I do. And what I do is . . . eh . . ." He inserts and removes his pipe a few times.

"I guess I don't know what I do. Ha! Mostly I just sit around here. Where's here? I don't know. It's not important. I'm here and that's all there is to it. Wherever this is, it's pretty boring, truth be told. I used to be busy. I remember this one time I created a whole universe. Took me a week! That was some hard work. But I liked that seventh day. I got hooked on that seventh day. After that seventh day, I decided I was going to just keep on having seventh days for the rest of eternity.

"Every now and then I peek down at what I made, poke around in a few of the old hangouts. Cathedrals and such. But it's discouraging. People don't like me 'cause I'm old. But if I ignore what everyone is saying and just sit up here real quiet, I can remember the days when I was busy. And that makes me happy."

Frank Collins shuffles out while the music team starts to set up.

"That was him," I say to Wren. "The real God."

"Sure," she says, sort of laughing. Then she looks at my face. "You figured this out, right," she says.

"Figured what out," I say.

"None of them are God. That's the point." She frowns. "I wish he would be the real God, though. So I could picture who it is I'm mad at."

I stand. The room tips sideways, the sinkhole is squeezing, I sip air between my lips.

"Meet me at the canoe dock in half an hour," I say.

*   *   *

It's dusk. Tree frogs tuning up, fireflies drifting just above the grass. My sinkhole is on slow rotation, *you you* vibrating in my ribs. An accusation, not a request.

I walk past the elementary cabins and dining hall to the staircase leading down to the water. The stairs are roped off for the night. I unhook the rope and lay the slack end on the hillside, then walk down and take the path to the canoe dock, which is tucked beneath a rocky overhang surrounded by bushes and trees. The dock is totally hidden; you can't see it unless you're on it, or approaching it from the water.

I find the towel. Unroll it and remove the supplies. It's completely dark now. I light the candles and set the Advil bottle, New Testament, and flashlight beside the towel. I take off my shoes and sit on the edge of the dock, let my feet hang down into the water while I wait for Wren.

When she comes around the bend I can tell something's different. She seems sort of stiff, hunched up in her shoulders. Her hair is pulled back and she's changed into a short white skirt. I notice that one of her legs is brighter than the other—it takes me a minute to realize she's not wearing her compression stocking.

"Ohhh," she says, looking at the candles. "That's pretty." She twists and untwists a section of her ponytail.

"Thanks for coming," I say.

"No," she says. "I mean, sure. I wanted to." She stands there, shifting her weight, then comes over and sits beside me. She smells good—summery—a mixture of grass and sunscreen and something like cake frosting. I feel myself start to get hard. The sinkhole picks up some speed. I need to get this over with, I think. I realize I never thought about how to get things started.

"So I'm super-nervous," Wren says, turning to look at me. She's blinking a lot, keeps plucking at her skirt.

"Me too," I say. "I've been wanting to tell you about this thing for a really long time. Something that happens sometimes, in my chest . . ."

Wren's not looking at me. Her hand is moving around in one of her skirt pockets.

"When the doctor told me about the buildup of scar tissue, I knew I'd have to find out," she says. She draws this long, shaky breath. "I was hoping you'd be the one."

I feel her shove something into my hand. It's a wrapped condom.

Wren's crying now. "It's because of all the surgeries. The doctor said he wasn't sure if it would, you know. Fully *work* for me."

She takes my hand. "Please," she says. "I need to know."

The sinkhole is expanding, making it hard for me to speak.

"You don't have to wear the condom. I don't even know why I brought it."

"Wren," I say. "There's this thing in my chest—"

But she's pulling at the hem of her skirt, getting it higher and higher above her knees. Her breath is coming in sharp sucks. Then she's lying back on the towel, and the sinkhole is huge, it's squeezing my heart. *You, you, you.*

I lie beside her, take off my shirt, start to do the Gesture.

"Listen," I say. "I need your help."

She moves my hand away and starts kissing my chest all over, quick, light presses, and the sinkhole is tightening around my heart but now she's kissing my mouth and I taste salt, some kind of peppery spice. I reach for the Advil bottle.

"Use this," I say, handing it to her. "Pray for it to stop."

"For what to stop?" Her voice sounds far away, like I'm talking to her on the phone. She sits up and looks in the Advil container, sniffs. "Is this olive oil?"

"Say, *In the name of Jesus*," I tell her. My hand is circling, fast.

"Why do you keep doing that?"

"It's right in the middle," I say.

Wren reaches up and sort of smooths her bangs. Her hand is shaking.

"I thought you wanted—you brought candles."

"Even if you just breathe on it—" But she's pouring the oil out on her hands, she's reaching down inside my shorts, beneath my boxers, moving her fingers around till she finds the tip. I feel myself getting harder and the sinkhole is squeezing my heart so tight there are long pauses between beats. *You. You. You.* I hear a wail, the voice high-pitched like a girl's. I'm terrified the voice is mine.

I feel Wren sliding onto me, the tight squeeze of it. A door swinging open.

The sinkhole contracts, moves toward the door, starts to go through it.

"Don't let it get inside you," I say.

"But I want it to," she says, crying hard now.

"You don't understand," I say, but it's too late, I am *letting it happen*, the sinkhole is spiraling into a thin funnel and exiting through the door.

"I think—I think it's working," Wren says. She lets out a sob.

The sinkhole, narrow as a pencil, turns from black to gray to white, like rising smoke. And then everything is clear, the *you*s are gone and I can hear my heart beating in my ears.

I take a few deep breaths. I open my eyes and see Wren's

face, eyes closed, mouth open. Behind her the sky is a dark bowl pocked with stars.

"I think it's gone," I say.

Wren lifts up and falls onto her side, then curls into a ball at my feet. Her whole body is quivering like she's cold.

I sit up. The river looks flat and still as a lake, all that power churning just beneath the milk-spill light on its surface.

I put a hand on my chest.

Both hands.

"Wren," I say. "It worked."

"I knew you'd be the one," she says.

She covers her face with her hands.

"I'm so sorry," she says.

"No," I say, touching her leg, the one without the stocking. "That was amazing. You didn't even have to pray."

She sits up. "What are you talking about?" Her eyes are all squinty, her face so pale it's almost green, like a glow-in-the-dark toy.

"My sinkhole," I say. "You healed it."

Wren just looks at me. Her chin is shaking and she has a dark smear going down one of her cheeks.

"I thought you wanted to," she says. "I thought you liked me even though you knew about my surgeries."

I reach out to touch her hair, but she moves her head away.

I scoot closer to Wren, till we're sitting within inches of each other, face-to-face.

"I need you to feel something," I say.

I take one of her hands and lay it on the dime-sized spot of skin.

I cover her hand with both of mine and press.

DEMOLITION

1

The deaf man came to our church the first Sunday in Lent. A teenaged boy, wearing khaki pants and a bow tie, entered the sanctuary with him. They sat in the front pew. From behind we could see the bald spot on the man's crown, dark strands of hair slicked across. The boy was a foot taller than the man, with a wizened face and blond hair. We assumed they were father and son.

Of course we couldn't tell the man was deaf—not at first—though we did notice the attitude in which he sat, waiting for the service, head tilted back and tipped sideways as if discerning a far-off melody. When the organ prelude began, the boy lifted his hands and began to wave them back and forth. Immediately the man did the same. Thinking our visitors were of the charismatic persuasion (it was our custom to tolerate demonstrative worship, though we couldn't imagine our organist ever moving *us* to such displays), we grew uncomfortable and averted our eyes. But when Don Holdings stood to deliver the Welcome, the boy began to carve shapes into the air.

We'd never had a deaf person among us. We had the elderly hearing-impaired, but their disability was in the natural order of things. We gave them amplification headsets and watched them twirl the volume knobs at their ears.

After the service, a deacon offered the deaf man a headset to use the following week.

That won't do any good, the boy said. The silence inside his head is impenetrable.

The following Sunday some of us moved closer to the front. We were eager to watch the boy—his translator, it turned out—take sentences into his body and churn them out with his hands. We wanted to give our children a better view. During the sermon the boy mimicked the snap of scissors across his uplifted forearm for *shepherd*, for *sorrow* stroked the air with fluttering fingers as if brushing aside a beaded curtain. There seemed to be no turn of theological complexity the boy couldn't grasp, the hands, arms, and torso moving in single purpose without thought for the strange and, in another context, embarrassing motions they were performing.

Gathered in the foyer after the service, we said it was like watching an Olympic athlete, the kind of ease that made you *feel in your bones* you could get up off the couch and do a triple axel. It partook, we said, of the nature of holiness itself: one man giving of himself in surrender, the other receiving in gratitude.

2

It was during Communion the third week they visited that we saw Christ's foot tumble from the stained glass window at the end of the deaf man's pew. Those of us sitting nearby heard the soft *shink* of glass hitting the flagstone pavers.

We looked: Christ in the Jordan River, standing on one foot like a pelican; John the Baptist behind, shell aloft, about to pour. Underwater, Christ's remaining foot was the frozen turquoise of an Alaskan glacier, while his calf—also submerged, though separated from the foot by a thin strip of black lead—was a lambent sea green.

The missing foot was the size of a lime. Through the opening, a shaft of sunlight, spiraling with dust, shot into the nave and hit the cheek of the pastor's wife, who turned to locate the source of light.

The deaf man stood. The boy, in a stooped pose, also stood. The man signed to the boy, who turned to face us.

Corbett Earnshaw would like to make a confession, the boy said.

We realized we'd never asked the deaf man's name.

The organist stopped playing. The elders paused in the aisles, holding their silver trays.

Again the boy spoke:

Mr. Earnshaw would like to confess that he does not believe in Christianity, he has never believed in Christianity, and he will no longer be attending this church, nor any other church, for the indefinite future.

Corbett Earnshaw walked down the aisle and disappeared into the foyer. Two elders followed Earnshaw out of the sanctuary. The boy, still hunched in what now seemed an apologetic attitude, also left.

In the rear corner of the chancel, the organist began to play again, sotto voce.

3

We've been duped, we said. The deaf man's signing during hymns, his rapt attention to the translator—it had all looked so *heartfelt*. We agreed that using one's hands in worship gave the impression of spiritual earnestness; that had Corbett Earnshaw sung like the rest of us—head down, gripping the hymnal—we might have detected his insincerity.

A faction of our congregation, however, admired what Earnshaw had done. College students, graduate students, young singles. Some had body piercings and tattoos; many raised their hands during the Doxology and Benediction. These young men and women began to say—first among themselves, and then to the rest of us—that God worked in all sorts of ways, not only through what we considered our religious life; that God could use, for His own purposes, experiences that seemed anti-Christian, such as Corbett Earnshaw's leaving the church, an act that reflected the divine trait of honesty.

In leaving us, they said, Corbett Earnshaw was nearer to the real presence of Christ than he was before he left. In this sense, couldn't we view his act as an inspired one?

Many of us agreed, though we kept our opinions to ourselves until the Session of Elders declared an official position on the matter.

4

The Elders declared Corbett Earnshaw's confession and departure either a) evidence his soul was still unregenerate, or b) an act of apostasy, but only if his soul was—and this was doubtful—regenerate to begin with.

5

The Saturday after Earnshaw's departure, Heinrich Lotz, performing his weekly deacon's service of cleaning the sanctuary the evening before worship, found three fragments of broken stained glass on the aisle floor. He stooped to pick up the pieces, thick and opalescent, deep aubergine. He looked up: the sun in the window depicting Satan's temptation of Christ was missing. Christ's bare feet rested on the milk-colored dome of the temple roof. Heinrich held the pieces to the window, rotating them to determine fit. Then he peered through the open space.

For the first time in the thirty-two years he'd been a member of Lookout Mountain Church, Heinrich could see the view outside the nave's south wall.

He was looking at an enclosed courtyard, its narrow lawn dormant, the color of wheat. Across the lawn was the north-facing side of what had once been the rectory, but was now divided into rental units. Standing in the open window of a downstairs apartment was a young woman holding a cell phone to her ear. She was crying. For a moment Heinrich thought the girl saw him there, looking through the chink in the glass, and was pleading for his help. He wondered how long the girl had been living there, how long she'd been looking at the words *Thou shalt not tempt the Lord* spelled in reverse.

Heinrich returned to cleaning the pew cushions with a handheld vacuum.

When he finished it was dusk. The light in the sanctuary was dim. Heinrich checked the window again. This time the girl was sitting on the edge of her bed, naked from the waist up. Her nipples arced upward and outward, delicate pink.

The next morning, between services, in an alcove space used for private prayer, Heinrich confessed to an elder that he had succumbed to the temptation of lust and could no longer be of service to the church. He said that he had seen more of God's glory in the body of a half-naked girl than in the worship services of thirty years combined. That he would like to continue meditating on the glory of God in this fashion.

6

Today was Friday. Log day. Judy Aldrich, secretarial assistant to Pastor Tom Robinson, put on her headphones.

> Pastor's Log. Re: Stained glass. 3/18–3/22.
> Mon, 3/18: Stone tablets missing from panel near pulpit. Fragments located in aisle. Maintenance to replace.
> Wed 3/20: Missing: head of angel wrestling Jacob. Tablets repaired; cracks visible.
> Thu 3/21: Loaf from feeding of 5,000 missing. Pieces located beneath pew.
> Fri 3/22: Missing: Burning bush. Six apples from Tree of Life. *Judy* (she jumped), *please add an agenda item for Monday's Session meeting: discuss hiring expert to evaluate integrity of windows.*

7

The SGAA-certified glazier flew down to Chattanooga from J&R Lamb Studios in New Jersey. Her evaluation was brief. The lead cames, she said, were *admirably* bearing the weight of the glass. The H-strips were thick and solid, as was the casing.

No need to re-lead or caulk the perimeter or horizontal solder joints—the glass fit perfectly into the grooves.

But what you have here is interesting, she said.

She was standing in front of Noah's ark, running her fingers along the lead ridges between rainbow colors.

Interesting, Pastor Robinson said. And dangerous.

I meant the placement, she said. Usually in these historic churches it's Old Testament on one side, New Testament on the other—your typical poor man's Bible. Here you've got the empty tomb smack up against Jacob's ladder.

I believe the windows were commissioned that way on purpose, Robinson said. To convey the unity of the Testaments.

In any case, the glazier said, you need to talk to a contractor. Because I'm thinking, *foundation.*

8

Teddy Ellison, General Contractor, Expert Stonemason, drove in from Mentone, Alabama. When the eval request from the church came across his desk he'd pounced. A sure-bet gig: in a building as old and large as the one up on Lookout, there were bound to be foundation troubles—leakage, settling, cracks in the mortar, the like. Some nice cash in reinforcement work, or—with luck—a complete substructural redesign. The South was getting old. It was a good time to be in the restoration business.

In the cool basement beneath the sanctuary, holding a pencil flashlight between his teeth, Teddy wrote at the top of his clipboard:

Lookout Mountain Church. Erected 1898. Designed by Chattanooga architect R. H. Hunt. Foundation: granite grade stone set with quick lime mortar in a tight rubble design.

Then he went down his usual checklist:

1. Are there any dislocations—above grade loose stones exposing the foundation to splashing roof runoff? *[none noted]*
2. Any obvious areas of discoloration? *[none noted]*
3. Any bulges created by frost, water leakage, or vehicle loading? *[none noted]*
4. Any obvious cracks in the mortar? *[noted: eight cracks of negligible size/import; recommend polyurethane fill]*
5. Have there been any interruptions (e.g., removing stones from the structural walls without adding lintels)? *[noted: lintels in place where windows added; no loss of structural integrity observed]*

Teddy stared at the list.

Then, because in twenty-four years of construction work not one building—certainly not one as old as this church—had ever passed inspection with such *absence of inadequacy*, he added one more entry:

6. *[!!]*

9

In the interest of safety, and to prevent further damage, the Elders hired a team from the Igneous Glass Company to remove, for the time being, all stained glass from the sanctuary windows. Using soft-nubbed medical reflex hammers, six artisans and their apprentices tapped out the glass. Each piece

was sealed in its own bubble-wrap baggie; the baggies laid
between sheets of foam eggshell; the sheets of eggshell stacked
in lined crates roughly the size of coffins. The crates were then
labeled by content—*Daniel w/ lions, Mary w/ Gabriel, Elijah
w/ chariot*—and shipped to a temperature-controlled storage
facility in Atlanta.

10

God's judgment, some of our members said. Perhaps there
are some who, like Jonah, need to come up from hiding in the
bowels of their ships.

With no shortage of churches in Chattanooga (none of
them dealing with such *spookiness*), many began attending
services off the mountain.

By the first of May, our membership had dropped from
150 to 78.

Only a handful of us—the faction that had favored Corbett Earnshaw's departure, and those of us who agreed with
them—said the missing stained glass was a *gift*. With only
the lead outlines remaining, the familiar Bible stories were
now articulated in three dimensions: yellow-greens of spring
maple and silvered sprays of pine; fade-to-gray of cloud;
blue sky beyond. Could it be, we said, that in this fusion of
the ancient stories with present-day creation, God meant
to reawaken our childhood sense of mystery? Hadn't some
of us noticed, lately, gilded horizon lines at the borders of
things, a refracted spangling along the edges of sidewalks?
Hadn't others of us sworn we'd felt a finger brush the backs of
our necks or calves while we stood loading our dishwashers,

brushing our teeth? Perhaps, we said, God wanted gently to remind us of the world we'd forgotten about, the *other* Nature hovering behind our own; and though we couldn't see it—not yet—we grew increasingly certain it was there, just in front of us, waiting on the other side of a one-way mirror, breath fogging up the glass.

Unwilling to abandon the church, the remaining leaders—an elder, the organist, and Robinson himself—formed a Committee for the Reestablishment of Order. Their first recommendation: the immediate removal of Sunday services to the windowless Fellowship Hall. But we refused to move. For the first time we could see each other worshipping in the natural light. Breezes fluttered our skirts and chucked our collars up under our chins. Through the empty lead cames drifted scents of honeysuckle and wisteria, mown grass, grilled fish. We could hear weed trimmers, children's laughter; the whir of a moped, the drone of an airplane.

The insects became a nuisance. We purchased twelve 40-watt Flowtron bug zappers, each with half-acre coverage, and hung them from shepherd's hooks outside the windows. During prayer we could hear the faint *zing* of mosquitoes, the louder *pops* of beetles and flies. At the end of each service, dead moths clung to the electric coils like wet leaves.

When a flight of swallows began nesting, we decided it would be best to remove the beams. Without the support of the beams, the roof, too, would have to go. But this was no great loss. Many of us—though we'd never said so to one another—had begun to long for total open-air worship.

Authenticity, some of us said. Our unnamed longing, revealed.

Revival, others said. The first breath of a New Great
Awakening.

The remaining leaders declared what was happening not
an Awakening, but an Insurrection.

Pastor Robinson was the last to go.

11

The question for those of us who remained (forty-seven in all)
became the walls themselves: once we took out the support
beams and lifted off the roof, did we, in fact, need them?

The sanctuary was three stories high, constructed of mor-
tared stones from a long-defunct quarry halfway down the
mountain. The stones had been carried up in wagons pulled
by teams of oxen, the Whiteside Turnpike laid in 1867 for this
purpose: sixty-eight curves, six reverses, three "W"s, a double
"S," one hairpin.

We asked Teddy Ellison to give us a bid on the demolition.
Outside the sanctuary, Teddy ran his hands over the stones,
his eyes wide.

Do you realize what you've got here?

We said we didn't.

Pick any ten-by-ten section of this wall. What's the smallest
stone you see?

We pointed to stones eighteen inches in diameter.

Do you know what that means? Teddy asked.

We said we didn't.

No plugs, Teddy said. Every stone laid out on the ground
and fitted together like a puzzle. *Before construction.*

He paused.

No one builds like this anymore, he said.

We allowed ourselves a moment to regret living in an aesthetically denigrated era, one in which the use of plugs was no longer considered a blight on artistry.

Then we called in the wrecking crew.

12

We scheduled the demolition for the first Saturday in June. We'd planned on staging a ceremony: a short speech followed by a ceremonial cutting of the velvet dossal curtain hanging behind the altar. But in the hush of the morning—dripping from drainage pipes, hum of idling machinery, parachute cotton and whirlybird maple seeds twisting down around us like slow-falling meteors—we decided a ceremony would be a mistake. Words, we said, would only scum things up.

We waited in the empty parking lot of the church across the street, holding the hands of our children, who wore the plastic toy hard hats we'd purchased for the occasion. The empty sanctuary rose before us, red *Danger* tape circling its perimeter. Yellow lights flashed atop striped barricades. Machinery crouched around the building—bulldozers, articulated haulers, excavators, backhoes, cranes. Two fire trucks to hose down the dust.

Teddy Ellison stood beside a rumbling excavator. He looked at the driver in his elevated cab, who gave him a thumbs-up.

Teddy raised an orange flag, let it fall.

The excavator reared back, its bent arm blindly probing the air. Then it straightened and—with sudden, delicate precision—plunged.

13

Corbett Earnshaw returned the second day of the demolition. This time—with the crashing rock, the roar of machinery, the ground beneath us vibrating—we knew why he came. He had a new translator with him: a girl, about twenty, with long brown ringlets and pale skin overlaid with a light sheen of moisture. She wore a white skirt and a bandanna halter that pressed her breasts flat against her torso. Her clavicles were prominent and straight as a crossbar; her bare feet turned out when she walked.

I'm Claire, she said.

Earnshaw wore loose jeans and a black T-shirt. The hair at the back of his head had grown long enough to cinch into a ponytail, a question mark at the nape of his neck. He seemed unable to take his hands off the girl. When she signed to him, he touched her face and bare upper arms, brushed her cheek or the side of her breast. And though we guessed he was at least twenty years Claire's senior, we couldn't blame him for wanting such loveliness in his eyes and hands.

Now, standing before us on the lawn of the Baptist church where we sat watching the demolition, Earnshaw and Claire signed to one another. Earnshaw held on to Claire's waist while she spoke, her hands graceful. She rose up on her toes *en pointe*. For a moment we thought Earnshaw might lift the girl over his head.

Claire turned to us.

He wants to lie down in the street, she said. He wants to feel it in his body.

With each rumble as the stone shattered and collapsed into piles, we watched Earnshaw's prostrate body shiver. He extended his arms and pressed his face into the asphalt, hands clasping and unclasping as if clutching sand. Claire lay on her back beside him. She took his hand and placed it on her stomach, sliding her own hand beneath his, her fingers curling words into his palm. Then she laid her hand on top of Earnshaw's, which began to spell in turn, making Claire's knuckles tilt right, left, right.

Word becoming flesh, we thought, dust from the crumbling stone filling our nostrils. A secret dialogue, skin-on-skin—we would have given anything to hear what they were saying.

14

The church came down like an opening book. The debris fell outward, as if some center binding had heaved itself up, flinging back the walls. Bulldozers pushed a mixture of dirt and pea gravel into the rectangular basement, burying old doors and windowpanes. Workmen hosed the backfill at six-inch intervals. Steamrollers packed the layers down. Fresh asphalt was laid over the footprint, hot and black, smelling of burnt charcoal.

Two weeks after it began, the demolition was complete. Those of us who continued to visit the site noted two things: 1) a silence beneath the daytime drone of cicadas and beady nighttime noises of crickets and tree frogs; and 2) the expanse of blue above the tree line, the place the cross used to sit now just a point in the sky.

It was Daryl Lotz—Heinrich's grandson, a philosophy major at Westminster College—who suggested we begin holding our Sunday services at the Natural Bridge Park. The Natural Bridge was a sixty-foot-long, fifteen-foot-high granite arch suspended between two boulders in a ravine below Bragg Avenue. Beneath the arch was the cave with a once-famous spring, now a slow trickle of water from a crack funneling deep into the rock. The Victorian Spiritualists believed the iron-rich water—chalybeate—would reverse the aging process, and in 1885 began importing mediums to distribute the water and contact the dead (Chattanooga was then a town filled with the newly-wealthy who had lost relatives in the Civil War—plenty of cash for longer lives and investment advice). The Sunday after the demolition, we walked down Bragg to the trailhead.

Earnshaw led the way. Why we allowed him to lead—why we followed—we couldn't say, though we suspected it was because he seemed to have obtained, through a grace given only to persons lacking one of the five primary senses, a higher knowledge about the workings of God and the nature of the Universe. There was also something both thrilling and unnerving in his relationship with Claire. We'd learned she was nineteen—twenty-seven years Earnshaw's junior. Whether she had access to the same secrets as Earnshaw or only translated them we didn't know. We followed them down the trail, moving branches, pinching burrs off our clothing.

The path opened onto a clearing in front of the rock arch, beneath which sat three picnic tables. Earnshaw stood on one of the picnic benches, facing us, hands loose at his sides. Claire stood beside him. The rest of us found places on mossy boulders or patches of dirt.

For a full minute Earnshaw was silent. Then he drew back his arm, closed his eyes, and—using a twisting, backhanded maneuver, as if throwing a curveball—punched himself in the jaw.

Shame, Claire translated.
Earnshaw rubbed his fist, hard, into the palm of his hand.
Erase, Claire translated.
No—*Eradicate*, she said.

15

Onlookers—former members, residents, casual tourists—hiked
down the trail. Some stayed in the woods surrounding the
clearing; others approached and made hostile remarks.

How can you call yourselves a church without a building?
they asked. Without a church home?

Our bodies are His home, we said.

Miles Phillips showed up with the word *Home* tattooed on
his neck; his girlfriend had the same tattoo on her wrist. *Home*
began to appear in various places on each of our bodies—feet,
calves, hipbones, forearms. Marguerite Dean's mother had tem-
porary *Home* tattoos made for the children, who transferred
them onto their foreheads. From a distance, they looked like
tiny symmetrical bruises.

To avoid questions, we began to meet in secret, after dark.
We brought lanterns, cookstoves, tents, sleeping bags. Shared
food and clothing. Took turns buying cases of bottled water,
storing them in the cave—where, we'd discovered, Earnshaw
and Claire had taken up residence.

16

Darkness. We sat in the clearing, our children asleep in our laps.

Earnshaw raised a hand and spelled. Claire began to
translate:

For a long time, you have been told that the entry into eternal life will come about either after you die or when Christ returns. You have been told that humans might *begin* the journey toward individual perfection, but will never reach it in this life. That only one individual—a God-man—was able to reach a state of sinlessness while on earth. And that by some invisible, inconceivable act of substitution, you too will be counted as sinless, despite the persistence of sin, if only you believe it is so.

But the truth, Earnshaw said, is that we can enter eternity here, on this planet. *Of our own volition.*

Our ears burned. We felt we should contradict him.

Your calling, Earnshaw said, is to make this happen in yourselves, so that the planet might be renewed and evil might cease to exist.

Impossible, someone said.

Claire made a hang-ten sign with her right hand and lowered it into her left palm.

Earnshaw signed rapidly.

It isn't a matter of changing one's *behavior*, Claire translated. It's a matter of changing one's *perception*.

Sin is sin, someone else said. How can we perceive anything else?

Again Earnshaw punched his cheek, drove his fist into his palm.

Eradicate shame, Claire said.

It takes practice, she said.

17

We practiced. Julia Reynolds confessed her addiction to girl-on-girl pornography; Flynn Jamison admitted that every time she had sex with her boyfriend she imagined it was her father; Roger Bantam said he had been cheating on his wife for a year, having sex with both women and men, some of whom were strangers, in public restrooms; Bill Leavis said he euthanized his dying wife, fed her eight syringes of morphine when the hospice nurse left even though his wife tried to refuse the drug, clamping down on the syringe with her teeth so that Bill had to squeeze her jaws until the syringe tumbled onto her sheeted chest; Thom Daniel said he once tried to drown his four-year-old autistic son in the backyard swimming pool while his wife was at the gym but had chickened out when he felt the child's limbs go slack, so he yanked him up and laid him on the deck and gave him mouth-to-mouth until the boy choked up the water in his lungs and when his wife came home and found Thom sitting in a pool chaise snuggling the boy, who was wrapped in a towel, she thanked him for spending *quality time* with their son, said she sometimes *didn't have the patience,* and began to cry, and now the boy was nine and unable to speak and wore diapers and every day during his lunch hour Thom locked his office door and made lists of ways to bring his son's fruitless life to a humane end.

Sound and fury, Earnshaw signed when the confessions ended. The very word *confession* is meaningless. There is no sin—there is only forgetting that sin does not exist.

We wept.

We reached out to touch his ankle where it showed beneath the hem of his jeans.

Who are you, we asked.

Earnshaw made a "V" sign on his neck, then flicked his fingers toward us as if brushing crumbs from beneath his chin.

The voice of one—*proclaiming,* Claire said.

18

The Christian, Earnshaw said, may perhaps best understand things from the standpoint of evolution.

Midnight. We were gathered around a small fire inside the cave, our bare feet stretched toward the flames.

If man evolved from lower types of life, Earnshaw said, then why haven't we reached the Next Step? When is the Thing After Man going to appear? Think of what came before humans appeared on earth. Huge, heavily armored creatures. If anyone had been watching the course of evolution, he would have predicted bigger creatures, heavier armor. But what did Nature give us?

Men, we said. Women.

Comparatively tiny beings, Earnshaw said. Naked, defenseless—with brains to master the planet.

As we continue to evolve, Earnshaw said, we should expect not just change, but a new method of producing the change.

Earnshaw stood and signed with large, cutting strokes.

The next stage in evolution, Claire translated, will not be a stage in evolution at all; evolution itself as a method of producing change will be superseded.

Haven't we read this in our theologians? we asked.

Your theologians, Earnshaw said, have told you that the Next Step is the transition from being God's creatures to his sons. They have *seen through a glass darkly*. In fact, the Next Step will occur only when we recognize sin as an illusion.

Earnshaw punched his cheek, twisted his clenched fist in his palm.

Claire did not need to translate.

19

Who will be the first to undress? Earnshaw asked.

Now that he'd spoken the words, we realized it was the question we'd been waiting for all along.

Is this not the reason you have taken down your building, Earnshaw said, to look upon His creation without barrier?

Sarah Taylor, a single mother, thirty-six, stood. We closed our eyes, or looked down into our laps, until Earnshaw reminded us that the term *modesty* was a euphemism for shame.

Sarah's body, Earnshaw said, is half the mystery of God's nature. On *mystery* he curled his index finger against his forehead, furrowing his brow as if perplexed. Our children mimicked the gesture.

Sarah pulled off her shirt and unhooked her bra. She took off her jeans, so baggy and outdated the lace thong she wore startled us (but only for a moment) like a cussword. We suppressed the urge to cover our children's eyes; they hid their faces anyhow.

Sarah bent over and slid out of the thong, then stood and lifted her hands. When she began to sing the Doxology, we joined in, some of us also removing our clothing, though we stayed in the darkness outside the circle of firelight, chiding ourselves for being trapped by the current of modesty, a weakness we would teach ourselves—and our children—to overcome.

20

Two nights later, when we arrived at the cave, Sarah was already undressed. She sat with her knees pulled up, arms crossed over her breasts.

We removed our own shoes, shirts, pants. Our children played in the clearing, or borrowed flashlights to explore the woods, or drew with sidewalk chalk on the smooth surfaces of the granite and limestone. They refused to enter the cave.

Claire spoke to Sarah in a low voice, Earnshaw signing beside them, using small hand gestures as if whispering. Sarah lay back, letting her knees fall open, the soles of her feet pressed together. We closed our eyes.

She is half the mystery of God, we heard Claire say. We should look upon His mystery without shame.

We forced ourselves to look upon the mystery, the gap-lipped pinkness.

Who will be the first to enact the mystery of God, Earnshaw said, with Sarah? To show us, in the flesh, His total nature, male and female combined?

We were silent.

Even Christ spoke in parables, Earnshaw said. Sexual union is not only profoundly natural, but inevitable as a means of expressing the desired union between God and men.

A young man stood—Daryl Lotz, the philosophy student. I will enact God's mystery, he said.

Sarah's breasts draped the sides of her torso. Daryl came forward, knelt between her legs, unzipped his cargo shorts. He put a hand on himself and moaned. If Sarah made any sound, we couldn't hear it.

Daryl lowered himself till his body was covering Sarah's. Then, abruptly, he crawled forward till his hips hovered just above her face.

Body of Christ, broken for you, he said, placing himself on her outstretched tongue.

21

Together each night, under the cover of darkness, we discovered the sacramental nature of oral ministrations. The men laid themselves on our women's tongues—and on one another's tongues—in humble acts of devotion. The women straddled waiting mouths, heads thrown back, eyes closed.

When we finished, we turned to Earnshaw (who watched, but, along with Claire, did not participate):

The Next Step, we said. Have we taken it?

Go further, he said. Think of the Son on the cross, the Father who put him there—dominance and subjugation also two sides of God's total nature.

We went further. We accepted everyone, endured everything, turning one another over and over again, our faces streaked with dirt and tears.

22

In the aftermath of our rituals, a stillness would overtake us. And in the stillness, our limbs entwined, we began to understand that the entrance to eternity lay not in the gratification of the body's desires, but in their denial. We discovered that on the other side of sexual union was a period of lucid stasis in which white roads unfolded on the insides of our eyelids, bright shapes rising on either side like backlit skyscrapers. In the stillness we allowed our thoughts, like clouds, to drift among the tops of the buildings. We *observed* our thoughts (*Where are our children?*) and watched them dissipate.

In the stillness we felt the approach of the infinite.

23

With fall coming on, in the sunlight of the clearing, leaves shrinking into bright stipple above us, we practiced being Awake to the Present Moment. Some of us mastered being still for such long periods of time that when we moved a limb we had to disentangle it from the kudzu. Lovely, we said, observing the coiling vines, purple flowers dotting our forearms, shins. Our children stayed in the woods. Sometimes we glimpsed them in the trees, peering down at us, hair hanging loose, obscuring their faces.

24

Former members and clergy from around the city sent letters. On Mondays, the postman carried them down the trail, leaving them on a flat rock beside the mouth of the cave. We knew what was in the letters, especially those that arrived certified mail.

There were legalities.

The South would not long stand our *debauchery*.

25

Have we reached it? we asked each day. Claire no longer translated. Our voices, weak from disuse, were difficult to distinguish from the wind in the Georgia pines.

26

Sarah Taylor achieved stillness for five days straight. We rolled our heads to admire the placid way she allowed insects to scurry across her naked torso. When on the sixth morning it was discovered she was dead, we observed her body as it appeared in the early morning light: face gone blue, eyes sunk in their sockets, cheekbones thrusting out. We covered her feet, legs, and torso with earth and rocks and leaves. When we reached her face we noticed her parted lips, tongue swollen and protruding slightly, her brow furrowed, as if death had caught her in the act of tasting something she didn't like.

27

When Earnshaw disappeared (Claire said he had *moved on* but many of us said that, like Elijah, he had been *caught up*), we knew we'd arrived.

Thank you, we whispered into the space around our heads.

We returned to stillness. Watched the letters pile up at the mouth of the cave.

28

A restlessness remains in our children. They gather fallen branches and carry them into the surrounding woods. We suspect they're building shelters. In the afternoons we hear a rhythmic scraping, the sound of dirt floors being swept. We conjure images of their improvised hovels, their rudimentary fires; we imagine the ways in which they might divide their tasks—food-gatherers, fire-tenders, storytellers. At night we hear them singing, hymnlike strains bright with major harmonies.

All of this we will teach out of them.

How we'll lisp to our children—softly, softly.

When they come back from the world they've made without us.

Holy Ground

Goodbye, I say to my husband and children. I'm going for a run and won't be back for a few days.

They're sitting on the couch in the formal living room, all five in a row, arranged oldest to youngest.

I mean it, I say. Days. Maybe weeks. You might miss me.

The four-year-old starts to cry, and the sister beside him puts an arm around his shoulders.

Go on, my husband says. We'll be waiting for you when you get back.

Where? I ask. Where will you be waiting?

Here. We'll stay on this couch until you come back. You won't have to worry about our physical safety.

Thank you, I say, kneeling to kiss the tops of his leather loafers. I've needed to do this for quite some time.

You have our support, he says. He elbows the daughter at his side, who nods and elbows her brother. This continues down to the youngest.

I go into the kitchen and fill the center pocket of my anorak with protein bars, then remove a water bottle from its rack in the fridge—this I will carry in my hand. I slide my toothbrush down into my sock like a splint. I set the alarm, lock the back door, and head straight for God.

The church parking lot is empty except for the cars in the spaces marked *Seniors Only*. It's Thursday evening, night of the Caring and Sharing Dinner for Ambulatory Seniors. I jog into the courtyard—the maple in the center of the grass is topless, sparse yellow leaves on its lower half—and through the double doors of the Fellowship Hall.

White-haired folks are seated around glowing candlelit tables. The women wear red hyacinths on their wrists or tucked behind their ears. Old men in sweaters make eyes at the women. They raise their wineglasses with bent hands. A wiry chap in stocking feet plays footsy with the bright-eyed woman beside him, her nostrils flaring around an oxygen tube.

The shoeless man notices me and winks. Like to join us? he asks.

No, thank you, I say. I've come to see Pastor Robinson.

God bless the man! he says, raising his goblet.

God bless him! say the others, glasses aloft. One woman drops hers, spattering the sweater of the gentleman next to her.

The wiry man drinks until his goblet is empty. You oughta heard his sermon Sunday, he says to me. Man preached salvation by grace using the text of Abraham and Isaac . . .

I know, I say. I was there.

Remarkable synthesis of the Old and New Covenants, the man says. Theology like that makes you want to get up and dance. Makes you want to mount up with wings like an eagle!

He takes a large sideways bite of ham, showing all his teeth when he chews.

How lovely, the women exclaim. Marvelous, those strong teeth.

Baking soda—straight from the box since I was seven, the man says.

I find Pastor Robinson in his office.

I hear you're leaving us, he says.

I kneel and encircle his calves with my arms. Can I do this with impunity? I ask, looking up at him.

He strokes my hair.

I mean, it's nothing against you, or your theology. I'm just worn out from *thinking* all the time.

I place my cheek on his knee. He is a large man and his thighs are soft. His gray wool pants sprout tiny white threads like curling hairs.

How do I worship with heart, soul, mind, and strength? I ask, when I keep privileging the mind and saying no to the body?

His legs make a sharp movement; I'm forced to sit back on my knees.

It's not what you think, I say. I only want to go down and do some work among the poor.

Then, because I have decided to be honest in this endeavor, I say, I would like to confess something, before I go.

He pulls my head back onto his knees.

I breathe in, once. Long exhale. And I say: I've been having an affair with a man I've never touched. For almost a year now.

An emotional affair, Pastor Robinson says.

Yes. Physical, too.

He frowns.

The sharing of ideas, I say. The composing, together, of an elaborate fiction.

Pastor Robinson recedes into the cushions behind him.

It's why I'm leaving, I say. I'm afraid if I don't get away it's going to undo me.

Leaving isn't the answer, he says.

Listen, I say. There are days I let my six-year-old surf the net, unsupervised, while I compose e-mails in the den. Nights I put the children to bed, come downstairs, and realize I can't remember a single thing any of them said to me.

Repent, Pastor Robinson says. Before it's too late.

I'm no longer making love to my husband, when we make love, I say.

Tell him, he says. Let him see your remorse.

I *used* to feel remorse.

You'll lose everything, he says. Wind up inside a living hell.

Oh, I've been living there a while, I say.

Pastor Robinson shrinks farther back into the cushions.

I'm not the person I thought I was, I say. I might be capable of anything.

I can recommend several good marriage counselors.

I need to get some distance from it, I say. See pain and suffering, poverty and loss. Serve the poor in some way.

Immerse yourself in charitable works? Attempt to overcome evil with good? You know better. Your graduate studies in divinity . . .

They're doing me no good in this case, I say. Look, it's a last-ditch effort. But can I have your blessing?

There will be healing only in renunciation, he says. In turning away from sin and toward God.

I don't have it in me, I say. Not yet. Do I have your blessing?
Pastor Robinson stands. His oxfords are worn and rumpled
leather, tiny pinprick holes patterning the toes.

I will pray for you while you're gone, he says. At length.

Running downhill on Hardy Road is the easy part. It's twilight,
the sky blue-gray with only the planets out. The street is wet
from the day's rain and the air smells like damp leaves and
wood smoke.

I turn onto Fleetwood, run past Rock City with its ten thousand Christmas lights already glittering along the Enchanted
Trail. I run past the Witch's Cabin Hotel, where Fleetwood
begins to circle the Lookout Mountain golf course.

Here is something I've discovered: if you cut through the
bramble and thick Chinese privet hedge across from the ninth
tee, you will find yourself on an outcropping of rock above
Flintstone, Georgia. Chattanooga to the left, Georgia directly
in front of you, to the right Alabama picking up where the
mountain begins to drop off. Everywhere, ridges cresting and
cresting all the way to the Smoky Mountains in Kentucky, the
Blue Ridge in North Carolina. Some mornings a cottony fog
lies over the ribbed land below, and to look across it is like
looking out across the sea. But on a clear day, they say you
can see seven states. No one believes it, but the claim brings
tourists up to our town.

I cut through the hedge in the place where I've been forging an opening and run out onto the rocks. Depressions in the
limestone, filled with rainwater, look like tidepools. In a cleft
between the rocks is a Moses bush, leaves brilliant red in the
near-dark. *Take off your sandals, Moses, for the place where
you are standing is holy ground.* Usually, when God shows up

in the Old Testament—a theophany—people die. Or else they fall facedown as *if* they're dead. There are two exceptions: Moses and Hagar.

Hagar, where have you come from, where are you going?

I stand, breathing long and deep, the watery lights of Chattanooga coming on below me. I consider the city. I want to see it like this, whole and from a distance; to see, before I go down, the signatures of the things I am about to read.

Running down a mountainside is hard. There is much slipping at a sideways angle. Your bottom gets wet and all exposed skin is painfully raked. It is not good exercise.

When I reach the base of the mountain, I eat half a protein bar and drink some water. The backs of my hands are crisscrossed with scratches, bleeding delicately, and I wipe them on my running tights. It's dark now and the wet asphalt reflects the orange streetlights. I take Broad Street all the way downtown, where, in the colorless window glass of the Sheraton Starbucks, my reflection stops me.

You look *hot,* babe, it says. You could pass for twenty-five.

Quintessence of dust, I say. The reflection turns to preen its backside, taut in black spandex.

I quote First Peter: The holy women of the past used to adorn themselves with a gentle and quiet spirit.

Women over fifty, the reflection says, are the only ones who believe that. I know why you're down here. You're looking for some action before you get old.

That's not it, I say. I'm trying to mortify all that.

Two college-aged boys—men?—are looking at me through the window. One of them is frowning; he watches me from beneath dark brows. He is beautiful—curved top lip, defined cheekbones, long hair in a ponytail. Small hoop earring.

You know they're checking you out, the reflection says.

Doesn't matter, I say. Now listen: Injustice. Oppression of the poor. Mistreatment of the uneducated.

You want the one with the earring.

Racial unity, I say. Single black mothers and well-to-do white mothers forging genuine friendships. In organic settings.

You sure that's all you're after? The reflection stretches its calves.

It's the only thing left that might still save me, I say, letting my shoulders slump.

The reflection jogs in place, then sets her watch and takes off down the sidewalk. I need to get my heart rate up, she calls back over her shoulder. Goodbye and good luck.

I run after her. Her blond ponytail sweeps the empty space just behind her neck. I sprint to catch up with her, because she is beautiful, and has an excellent stride.

I run east on Martin Luther King, between the old stone buildings on the UTC campus. My hip flexors burn and I can't feel the second and third toes on my left foot. I'm not sure I will make it all the way to the poor. I finish the protein bar.

College girls with slouchy bags strapped across their chests walk past me, checking me out. In the darkness next to the alumni house, a black man sits on a metal bench.

Hey, he says as I run past. Lady. I know you.

I stop and turn. I don't think so, I say.

Bring your kids to school there, Tuesdays. He points across the street to the Conservatory of Music.

Used to be true, I say. Won't be true again for a while.

He sits with his legs spread wide. He has a thick throat, shaved head, rings on all of his fingers.

I'm beat, I say. Mind if I sit down?

He moves and I sit beside him. Aren't you cold? I ask. I touch his bicep with my index finger. You should have a coat on.

Ain't never been cold, he says, pressing my whole hand against his warm armskin. Never in all my life.

I pull my hand away. You will be someday, I say. Better buy a coat while you're young.

He grabs the sleeve of my anorak. *Schorach ani wenowach, benoith Hierushaloim,* he says, and I flee, pulling out of my anorak, leaving it hanging there in his fist, heavy with the protein bars.

The business district is dark. Doors and windows are barred. I pass small white churches on almost every corner. Because I am exhausted, because my food is gone and the bottoms of my feet are numb, I ask the Baptists for a ride. I pick the Second Street St. James Missionary Church—its doors are open and the lights are on in the sanctuary. The pews are unfinished pine. There is no altar, only a long table with a white tablecloth, behind which are seated two white girls who look like college students.

Are you here for the interview? one of them asks. Her bangs are streaked red and orange.

I've come to help the poor, I say. Actually, I'd like to just sort of hang out with them. But I think I need a ride.

She does look exhausted, says the other girl, who wears her hair in long braids. Can't we just skip the interview? The girl has a teardrop hanging from the end of her nose. When she turns her head I see it's a silver nose ring.

How do we know what skills she has to offer? the girl with streaked hair says.

I'm good with kids, I say.

What else?

I can recite many of the Psalms besides the twenty-third. If you call out a verse, I can find it in under ten seconds.

Is that all?

I can recite the Westminster shorter catechism and explain Calvin's TULIP, though of course Calvin himself didn't use the five terms represented in the—

Is that *all*?

I can sort of read Hebrew. In fact there was a man who spoke to me in Hebrew just now. He quoted Song of Solomon . . .

Perfect, the girl with bangs says. Hebrew lessons in detox.

I'm sorry, the girl with braids says. We know it's not your fault.

Wait, I say. Are you looking for experiences of the supernatural variety? Once I saw the clouds open up in the shape of a five-point star.

It's a start, says the girl with bangs.

How's this? When I was little, maybe seven, I heard a voice outside my window one night. It was one voice but sounded like thousands of voices. Like the rush of a mighty waterfall.

The girl with streaked hair leans forward and readies a pen. And what did the voice say?

I wish I could remember, I say.

The two of them stand to leave.

For the third time that night I fall to my knees. Please? I say.

The girl with bangs turns and looks at me again. Well, now that's something, she says. On your knees like that. There might be a woman you could help.

Take me to her, I say. I've been running for such a long time.

The girl with streaked hair is driving. Her name is Jade. Her friend's name is Mimi. I'd be certain they were lovers if they weren't Baptists.

It's going to be crowded, Jade says to me. They're serving Thanksgiving dinner.

That's *today*? I picture my husband and children on the couch, microwave dinners balanced on their knees.

Next week, Mimi says from the backseat. Tonight's the meal with just the Oak Project girls. They kicked us out of the house so they could set up.

Jade looks at Mimi in the rearview, then at me. It's the name of our ministry, she says. The Oak Project. It's from that verse in Isaiah, about the oil of gladness—

They will be called oaks of righteousness, I say, a planting of the Lord for the display of his splendor?

Sweet, says Jade.

We turn into a neighborhood off McCallie Avenue. The houses are two-story bungalows, set close together, grimy, with gaping doors and warped porches. There are no streetlights. We park across from a house with Snoopy sheets hung for curtains. A girl squats on the stoop, while a young woman—older sister? mother?—picks through her hair with a comb. A cop car passes, slowly, its lights turned off; when we get out of the car the air is thick with cooking smells. An elderly black couple is walking arm in arm on the sidewalk next to us.

This is it, Jade says when we cross the street. She's standing in front of a clapboard bungalow with peeling paint, pale yellow in the light of the single bulb above the front door. A strand of small paper lanterns hangs from the porch rail.

When Jade opens the door I see green: the walls of the living/dining room are painted Granny Smith apple. There are no couches, no chairs or end tables, just a small computer desk pushed up against the side of the staircase, with a grouping of thick galvanized metal crosses arranged on the wall above the monitor, and three foldout metal tables covered in paper tablecloths with a fall-leaf print. The tables are set with paper plates, Styrofoam cups, clear plastic utensils. The centerpieces are pinecone turkeys with construction-paper feathers.

Around the tables are gathered women of every skin tone, black and white; mostly large-breasted, full-faced women wearing bright colors and big jewelry.

Whazzup, girls! Jade says.

Three women spring from tables, push back chairs, and run to us, throwing their arms around Jade and Mimi. Two of them hug me, their arms fleshy, their chests warm and soft. The third woman, her hair in cornrows, stands back and looks me up and down.

What'd you do with all our furniture? Mimi says.

Don't you worry about it, says one of the women. You all just sit down and let us serve you.

Why's *she* here? the woman with cornrows says.

She's going to hang with you all tonight, Jade says. We'll see how it goes.

She *ran* down the mountain to get here, Mimi says. I feel her squeeze my hand.

That's some legs she got on her, says a woman in a red velour sweatsuit. Girl, she says to me, you just sit down now and let us take care of you.

The women are neatly dressed. Several are wearing office attire—hose, pumps, silky button-down blouses. None of them look like the poor I imagined helping.

Jade takes me aside. That woman sitting alone, she says, nodding toward a table, lives at the shelter down the street. She's schizophrenic, but lithium keeps her stable, mostly. She likes to write. I want you to sit with her.

Do you mind if I get something to drink first? I'm not feeling very well.

Sit. I'll have Mimi bring you some tea.

I sit next to the woman from the shelter. Her hair is short, the color of rust. She smiles at me and I count three gold teeth. Her knees bounce.

I'm Eummenia, she says to me. It's an African name.

It's lovely. Say it again?

You-*men*-ia, she says. You got kids?

Four, I say. They're with their daddy.

I know how that goes, she says. I got a son named Zerah—that means brightness. He likes to draw. And a baby girl, Tanisha Starr.

Mimi fills my cup.

Do you mind if I put my head down for a minute? I say to Eummenia. I'm not feeling very well.

Niki! I hear Eummenia yell before I pass out. This white girl needs to *eat*!

The Oak Project women feed me. My head is on the table but now I'm looking sideways, my cheek resting on a soft black forearm. I feel long nails stroke through my hair—someone has removed my ponytail elastic—and I watch the platters pass: a turkey breast submerged in cornbread stuffing; glazed ham studded with cloves; pot roast with carrots and new potatoes; collard greens tossed with pearl onions; green bean casserole; sweet potato pie.

Eummenia is rubbing my back, her hand shaking like her knees. You just need something in your belly is all, she says. You just need your blood sugar up.

When my plate is full the women stand back to watch me. I take a bite of stuffing, then put my fork down. I can't eat this, I say. I feel too guilty. I'm pretty sure my kids and husband are eating microwave dinners.

Microwave dinners never killed a body, a woman says.

Plus—I look over at Jade and Mimi—I thought there might be work to do down here. I didn't think I would *accept* anything.

Ain't much of a friendship when only one's doing the giving, Eummenia says.

But I wanted to wash your feet.

Wash all you want, Eummenia says, they'll still be black.

I wanted to see suffering and pain, grief and loss. Something real. I start to cry and the women surround me, murmuring.

She been deprived of the real. She ain't never had a touch of the real, all her life.

We can tell you some things, Eummenia says. If you got the ears to hear.

I lean into her hand making circles through the fabric of my turtleneck, then raise my head to look at her. What is it you write about? I ask.

First question worth answering I ever been asked by a white lady, Eummenia says, and kisses me on the mouth.

After the meal the women push the tables against the walls, and everyone sits in a circle. Niki— the woman with cornrows—takes charge.

We're going to go around, she says, and tell what we're thankful for. Then Danielle's going to read from First John.

Ashley, a teenager with lashes like inky cursive and body glitter sparkling on her chest, goes first. I'm thankful I get to be around all y'all, she says. Cuz at home it's, like, all *negativity*.

An older white woman sitting next to Ashley, her gray hair cut in a shoulder-length bob, says, I'm thankful I made it to another Thanksgiving. And, she says, pointing with the index fingers on both hands to Jade and Mimi, for you two girls.

I'm thankful I live here, says a quiet girl, early twenties. I don't got to worry about getting hit by A. J.

I'm thankful I woke up today, Niki says. She looks down at her nails, which I notice are ripped and yellow, the skin on her thumbs torn raw. And I'm thankful I been off crack eighty-seven days now. She lifts her chin and looks at me. *Beat that.*

I'm thankful I got a job. This from the woman in the red sweatsuit.

When it's my turn I'm silent. Eummenia takes my hand. You just say something you're thankful for is all, she says.

I'm thankful to be here, too, I say. To have made it this far.

Danielle is the woman in the red sweatsuit. The text in her Bible is overlaid with blocks of color: lilac, mint, pale blue, a buttery yellow. She's sitting next to me and I can see the words in First John are mostly pink. The translation is modern, the language edgy and full of slang. *I'm not writing anything new here, friends. Whoever hates is still in the dark, doesn't know which end is up.* When she closes the book I see the cover: *The Rainbow Bible.*

Your Bible, I say to her. I've never seen that one.

It's a Rainbow, Danielle says. You want to look at it?

While the women talk about First John, I discover the blocks of color are a kind of topical code. Lilac for passages on *Baptism*, mint for *Salvation*, blue for *Grace*. The pink turns out to be *Love*; the buttery yellow, inexplicably, is *Satan*.

Sin is orange. I flip to Romans, where I know there will be entire chapters of orange.

Chapter five: when it's sin versus grace, grace wins, hands down.

Chapter six: think of it this way—sin speaks a language that means nothing to you, but God speaks your mother tongue.

Chapter seven: offer yourselves to sin and it's your last free act; offer yourselves to God and the freedom never quits.

The women start to sing. It's a praise chorus I've never heard, slow and repetitive. *I'm blessed, blessed, blessed*, they sing.

I close my eyes. I imagine the faces of my children, my husband. I pray for repentance, wait for it to fall over me like a benediction.

Blessed to know the Lord, the women sing.

So you're in, Jade says to me.

It's late, past ten. Jade, Mimi, and I are in the kitchen. The other women are moving the tables back, laying out dessert plates. Mimi is sitting on the counter beside the oven, wearing quilted mitts, waiting for the pumpkin pies to finish warming.

It's your honesty, Mimi says.

Our girls connect with that, you know? Jade says.

Listen, I say, not looking up, I'm no good to any of you.

You're tired, Jade says. You need to crash somewhere.

Can I tell you something? I say. When I was in ninth grade, I went home from a party with a guy I'd met an hour before. Stripped naked, threw myself facedown on his bed and begged him to teach me everything there was to know.

We all have our pasts, Mimi says.

The guy wouldn't touch me. Said he didn't need that on his conscience.

Protection of the Holy Spirit, Jade says.

No, listen, I say. My senior year I shoplifted a swimsuit—on a Young Life mission trip. The store owner caught me. I should have been arrested, but our team leader said, *Doctor's daughter, upstanding family.* When I paid for the suit, the owner wrapped it in pink tissue and tied it with raffia.

No one is righteous, not even one, Jade says.

That's not *it,* I say. *Listen* to me.

Mimi takes a pie out of the oven and slides it onto the stovetop.

I tried to fail a class in college. Eighteenth-Century Poetry. I never read a page or wrote a word. The professor gave me an A anyhow. She said she'd seen enough of my work to know that I would have earned an A.

Mimi holds up a forkful of steaming pumpkin. You've got to try this, she says.

I push the fork away; the pumpkin falls off the tines, makes a perfect circle on the linoleum. I've only had real sex with one man, ever, I say. I might need to let myself just *sin* for a while.

Go for it, Jade says. You'll still be God's girl.

In the living room, Eummenia is swaying in front of the computer desk.

198

Black woman's what I *am*, black woman's what I *be*, she repeats, a soft, blurry song.

She's writing poetry now, Niki says to me. She needs her meds.

I'll walk her home, I say.

Eummenia leads me to the shelter, The Shepherd's Arms. It's three blocks away, a large two-story house, part brick, part vinyl siding. She climbs an exterior staircase at the back and goes in through a door with an arched transom above it. Warm yellow light in the panes. I've never been inside a shelter. I want to follow her, but don't. Maybe there's some kind of visitor registration at the entrance.

In the front yard is wicker furniture, old and mildewed; also a birdbath and some beaten-down plastic toys. A balloon sags from the mailbox. In the porch light I can see a foil strand of letters hung over the front door: *Happy Birthday!*

When I climb the front steps I hear a low moan. In the corner of the porch, beside a trellis with rotting vines, sits a black man in a wheelchair. His skin is so dark I can't see his face until I come close. His hair looks like white powder sprinkled over his scalp. His head keeps tipping, then jerking back upright. He smells like urine.

Oovah, he says.

I sit across from him, on the railing.

You live here? I ask.

His tongue thrusts in and out of his mouth; he clamps his lips around it like it's the reed on a wind instrument and he's attempting to sound a note.

I'm visiting a friend, I say. Eummenia.

The man's body tips sideways, over the armrest on his chair. He pulls a lever and the chair starts to roll.

199

Dooah, he says.

I push him to the front door and open it.

Inside is a staircase, a room with two couches covered in plastic, and a warped Ping-Pong table. There are pamphlets on a rack beside a telephone. A piece of paper is taped to the wall, with names and extension numbers of residents—so many cross-outs I can hardly read it.

The man in the wheelchair motions toward the phone. I lift the receiver and dial Eummenia's extension.

Where you at? Eummenia says.

Downstairs, I say.

Two black men are sitting on one of the couches, smoking. The old man in the wheelchair rolls himself over to them. They look past him, blowing out smoke. On the other couch, which is pushed into a corner, a white girl is nursing a baby. She's young, a teenager. Her hair is two-tone, light on top, black underneath. She's wearing a tank top and pajama bottoms; her arms are tattooed with shapes that look like jagged mountain ranges.

God, she says. God Almighty.

She looks at me. Fuck it all, you know? she says.

Eummenia comes down the stairs. She's holding a cell phone.

Look at my baby girl, she says. Phone doesn't work but I still got my baby on here.

Eummenia shows me a video clip of Tanisha Starr. She's dancing the way a one-year-old dances—ducking her knees, arms bent out to the sides like wings. Eummenia plays the clip over and over: twenty-three seconds, tiny girl on a tiny screen. She's wearing just a diaper; a garbled rap song plays in the background.

Eummenia closes her eyes, throws back her head, starts to circle her hips.

Oh, oh, can my baby *dance*! she says.

The man in the wheelchair tips and jerks his head, moaning, his lips smiling around his thrusting tongue.

I envy these people. Wide-open suffering, their messes all hanging out. Lives boiled down to raw need—a near-holiness to it. And all of us driving our cars up and down the mountain— we'll go on forever trying to fool each other.

Your girl is a *fine* dancer, I say.

Then I start to dance with Eummenia. She grabs my waist and I hold on to her shoulders. I thrust my hips, circle my head around like she does. I sit down and take off my running shoes. My socks are bloody at the toes. I take them off, too. I watch the way Eummenia pounds the floor with her bare feet and try to do the same.

The men on the couch nod in time to the music, blowing smoke from their nostrils.

I could live here with you a while, I say to Eummenia when we stop dancing. It's the kind of place I need.

Extra bed in my room, Eummenia says. She sits down on the bottom step, panting. No sheets, though.

Now I've heard it all, the nursing girl says.

I walk over to the couch. Can I sit here? I ask her.

Whatever, she says.

I sit beside her. The baby is making little smacking sounds with its lips. I think about my own children, sitting on the couch at home. My husband will bring them blankets and cups of milk. He will make sure they don't watch too much TV and pray with them before they fall asleep.

I want to tell you a story, I say to the girl. Is that okay?

You'll tell it whether I say okay or not.

It's a short one, I say. It's the story I'll tell my children when they're your age. A woman leaves her home. She runs, long and far. And she finds out what, in all her life, is waiting when she goes back.

That's it? the girl says.

For now, I say.

Where're you going back to? she asks.

Lookout Mountain, Eummenia answers her.

Back up to rich people territory, the girl says. Back to holy ground.

Listen, I say. It's all holy ground.

RELATIVES OF GOD

The day I released you: summer in Minnesota, late afternoon. I was in Wal-Mart, standing in front of Granny Smiths, Galas, Jonagolds. My husband was in another aisle, picking out steaks, and I was thinking how this small town *lacked progress,* needed to *get with the times,* leave off genetic modification and crop dusting and join the renewable sustainable movement like the rest of the country—and I remembered a moment three years earlier, back home in Tennessee, when you and I were still in love. I was shopping in one of those organic markets and had you on the phone (it was like that, wasn't it—*had you*) and in the produce department I said, Best thing about fall: the Honeycrisp, and you said, I *adore* the Honeycrisp, and in the silence that followed, there was between us—what else to call it?—something like joy.

Later that day, my husband at work and the children in school, you listened while I brought myself to orgasm. It was the first time you were just the listener. When I cried out your childhood nickname, the one you'd told me your little sister used, you said, Don't ever call me anything else. It was the day my husband and I had argued about 69. I said I'd never liked it; that the simultaneous giving and receiving diluted the pleasure of both.

After we ate our Minnesota dinner, my husband and I took the children to Crescent Beach. We stood in the sand, watching the four of them slip around on the rock jetty, the setting sun turning the water a violent orange-pink. Our older son hopped from rock to rock, pulling off his shirt and shallow-diving into the lake, his boxers visible above the waistline of his madras shorts; his younger brother followed, cautious, all elbows and shoulder blades. The two girls sat at a safe distance from the water. We could hear the older sister talking the younger one out of jumping in. White T-shirt, she said, and the younger one nodded, grave, though her chest was still like a boy's.

My husband took my hand.

Look what we made, he said. We are relatives of God.

But I was picturing the children walking down the jetty and into the lake, one by one, oldest to youngest, the water closing over their heads. I was thinking how they would eventually disappear, how I would become resigned to their departure after years of hating the planet for spinning them away and leaving us more alone than we were before. I was thinking of Eve and her apple, or whatever kind of fruit it was; how she was driven by delight to share the taste with the one she loved, and it ruined them both, but God, knowing this in advance, loved them anyhow; and I knew, then, that I could forgive the boy and the girl on the phone three years earlier, the girl in the produce department holding an apple, saying, I think you would love this, the boy saying, Darling, I already do.

My husband put his arm around my waist. We watched our children. Our children, in glances, watched us.

Acknowledgments

For their enthusiasm, expertise, patience and grace, deepest thanks to my editor, Elisabeth Schmitz, and to my agent, Anna Stein. Thanks also to my agent's assistant John McElwee, and to Jessica Monahan, Deb Seager, Judy Hottensen, Morgan Entrekin, and the rest of the remarkable team at Grove.

For their guidance and encouragement, I'm grateful to my teachers: Doug Bauer, Amy Hempel, Jill McCorkle, Melissa Pritchard, and especially David Gates.

Thank you to the editors who, in one way or another, ushered these stories into the world: Robert Fogarty, Michael Griffith, Ronald Spatz, John Irwin, Mary Flinn, Michelle Wildgen, Sven Birkerts, Bill Pierce, William Giraldi, Jill Meyers, Wells Tower, Cara Blue Adams, Margot Livesey, Nick Flynn, Ladette Randolph, Catherine Chung, Meakin Armstrong, and David Lynn.

For their friendship, support and eyes on my work, thanks to Megan Mayhew Bergman, Tom Bissell, Elizabeth Crane, Mary Vassar Hitchings, Lisa Brennan-Jobs, Gayle Ligon, Dayna Lorentz, Nicola Mason, and Cal Morgan. Special thanks to Tim Liu.

I am indebted to the MacDowell Colony and to the Corporation of Yaddo for generously providing the time and solitude I needed to write many of the stories in this book. I'm also grateful to Wyatt Prunty, Kevin Wilson, and everyone else at the Sewanee School of Letters, and to Po Hannah, for bringing the magic lighter. Special thanks to Elena Quevedo for giving me a place to land in New York City.

For their love and support, thanks to my children, McKenna, Keaton, Hallie-Blair, and Hudson, and to my parents, John and Dani Utz. And to Scott: first reader, best reader, best friend of twenty-four years—you are my Home.

Note: The phrase "a wicked, unlovely, purely useful thing" in "Decomposition" is a variation of Will Barrett's description of the telescope case in Walker Percy's *The Last Gentleman*. Earnshaw's sermons in "Demolition" draw from the last chapter of C.S. Lewis's *Mere Christianity*. The Hebrew phrase in "Holy Ground" is from the Song of Solomon (by way of Joyce's *Ulysses*), and translates, "I am black yet comely, O ye daughters of Jerusalem."

Finally, I would like to acknowledge Sherwood Anderson, Barry Hannah, Denis Johnson, Gordon Lish, David Means, Steven Millhauser, Alice Munro, Tim O'Brien, Grace Paley, Mary Robinson, Christine Schutt, and Eudora Welty: Masters of the story form, all.